radio show

APRENDA INGLÊS COM UM PROGRAMA DE RÁDIO

elementary

Brian Brennan

Language Training Manager
International House Company Training, Barcelona

Tradução
Carlos Antonio Lourival de Lima
Egisvanda Isys de Almeida Sandes

© Difusión, Centro de Investigación y Publicaciones de Idiomas, S.L., Barcelona, 2009
© Martins Editora Livraria Ltda., São Paulo, 2011

Título original: *The Pons Idiomas Radio Show*
© **Fotografias** TRACK 04 Jiri Moucka/dreamstime.com, Bhe017/dreamstime.com TRACK 06 a Julio Rojas/flickr.com, b Vicky Brock/flickr.com, c Aaron Amat/dreamstime.com, d The County Clerk/flickr.com, e Sandra Forbes/flickr.com, f Prakhar Amba/flickr.com, g Rafael Moreno/flickr.com, h Peter Lorre/flickr.com, i Sir Iwan/flickr.com, j Mark Kobayashi-Hillary/flickr.com, k Kok Robin/flickr.com,
l viZZZual.com/flickr.com, monkey business/dreamstime.com TRACK 07 Dan Peretz/dreamstime.com, Ron Chapple Studios/dreamstime.com TRACK 08 jelena zaric/dreamstime.com, Andres Rodriguez/dreamstime.com, Elena Milevska/dreamstime.com, Robyn Mackenzie/dreamstime.com TRACK 09 Aleksejs Kostins/dreamstime.com, Kevin Renes/dreamstime.com TRACK 11 Les3photo8/dreamstime.com TRACK 12 1 blmurch/flickr.com, 2 Joe Mad/flickr.com, 3 Leonid Mamchenkov/flickr.com, 4 Mo Riza/flickr.com, 5 npslibrarian/flickr.com, 6 Peter Pearson/flickr.com, 7 Sam Saunders/flickr.com, 8 Scott Feldstein/flickr.com, 9 Tim Wilson/flickr.com, 10 Tracey R/flickr.com
TRACK 13 Fabrizio Mariani/dreamstime.com TRACK 14 Olga Semicheva/dreamstime.com, Orange Line Media/dreamstime.com TRACK 17 Sophie Asselin/dreamstime.com

Gravação: Blind Records, Barcelona
Produssom, São Paulo
Vozes: Juliet Allen, Margarita Alonso, Sioux Bean, Brian Brennan, Liam Chapman, Daniela Laudani, Stuart Lewis, Tunde Longmore, Peter Loveday, Dean Malcolm, Maria Elena McCarthy, Rob Merino, Lewis Parley, Gemma Sala, Karen Stigant (Espanha); Leandro Moura, Vanessa Keclaf (Brasil).

Músicas: © CD 1 TRACK 01 djbouly "Pop-expérience"/jamendo TRACK 02 Krayne "Cloud Nine"/jamendo TRACK 03 djbouly "Pop-expérience"/jamendo TRACK 04 Ultracat "Disco High"/jamendo TRACK 05 Josh Woodward "Dizzy Spell"/jamendo TRACK 06 djbouly "I would like to know"/jamendo TRACK 08 Mertruve "Introduction"/jamendo, Ultracat "Disco High"/jamendo TRACK 09 Beatjuice "Repeat"/jamendo TRACK 10 djbouly "Pop-expérience"/jamendo TRACK 11 Josh Woodward "Dizzy Spell"/jamendo, Still playing guitar "Nachtshatten"/jamendo TRACK 12 djbouly "Lost Melody"/jamendo **CD 2** TRACK 1 Frozen silence "Morning"/jamendo TRACK 2 Josh Woodward "Dizzy Spell"/jamendo TRACK 3 Predator "IQ 53"/jamendo TRACK 4 Peter Loveday "Here I am" TRACK 5 Williamson "2 percenter"/jamendo, OCD "Transparency (intro)"/jamendo TRACK 06 Josh Woodward "Darien gap"/jamendo TRACK 07 Josh Woodward "She dreams in blue"/jamendo TRACK 08 Josh Woodward "Darien gap"/jamendo TRACK 09 Josh Woodward "She dreams in blue"/jamendo TRACK 10 Josh Woodward "Darien gap"/jamendo

Design de capa: Patrícia De Michelis
Design de miolo: puntgroc

Publisher: Evandro Mendonça Martins Fontes
Coordenação editorial: Anna Dantes
Produção editorial: Alyne Azuma
Revisão técnica: Magda Lopes
Preparação: André Albert
Revisão: Denise Roberti Camargo

Dados Internacionais de Catalogação na Publicação (CIP)
(Câmara Brasileira do Livro, SP, Brasil)

Brennan, Brian
 Radio Show : aprenda inglês com programa de rádio : elementary / Brian Brennan ; tradução Carlos Antonio Lourival de Lima, Egisvanda Isys de Almeida Sandes. -- São Paulo : Martins Martins Fontes, 2011.

 Título original: The pons idiomas Radio Show (elementary)
 Inclui CD.
 ISBN 978-85-8063-003-9

 1. Inglês - Estudo e ensino 2. Rádio Show (Programa radiofônico) I. Título.

11-01718 CDD-420.7

Índices para catálogo sistemático:
1. Inglês : Estudo e ensino 420.7

Todos os direitos desta edição no Brasil reservados à
Martins Editora Livraria Ltda.
Av. Dr. Arnaldo, 2076
01255-000 SãoPaulo SP Brasil
Tel.: (11) 3116.0000
info@martinseditora.com.br
www.martinsmartinsfontes.com.br

INTRODUCTION

RADIO SHOW é o curso de inglês ideal tanto para iniciantes quanto para falsos iniciantes. A partir de um programa de rádio, você vai adquirir as competências de nível A1 e A2 do *Marco Comum Europeu de Referência* e, ao mesmo tempo, praticar de forma muito intensiva a compreensão oral, escutando os falantes nativos (britânicos, norte-americanos, australianos, canadenses etc.) que participam do programa. Projetado tanto para o autodidatismo quanto para a sala de aula, o curso propõe um aprendizado progressivo e comunicativo, bem centrado na aquisição do léxico.

O programa de rádio consiste em 17 seções, nas quais são tratados todos os tipos de temas (viagens, música, esportes, culinária etc.) que proporcionam diversos contextos de aprendizagem. Além do programa monolíngue, estão incluídas cinco faixas bilíngues, nas quais um professor nativo e uma estudante brasileira comentam e analisam os conteúdos linguísticos que apareceram nas diferentes seções.

Cada seção do programa corresponde a uma unidade do livro. As unidades incluem as seguintes partes:

LISTENING | Na primeira parte são propostas atividades cujo objetivo é avaliar a compreensão geral de cada seção. Também são incluídas atividades de compreensão mais específica, bem como outras centradas na descoberta da fonética e da entonação do inglês.

VOCABULARY | Inclui um conjunto diversificado de atividades destinadas à prática específica de questões lexicais que apareceram ao longo da faixa. Desta forma, há uma reflexão sobre os usos das palavras e sobre o contexto em que elas aparecem.

GRAMMAR | A partir de amostras da língua extraídas de cada seção, são apresentados seus aspectos morfológicos, sintáticos e funcionais, que são complementados por atividades corrigíveis pelo próprio leitor, estimulando a reflexão gramatical e a fixação dos diferentes aspectos tratados.

CULTURAL NOTE | Algumas unidades contêm textos culturais sobre o tema da seção que proporcionam informação complementar para a compreensão da faixa. Os textos incluem um glossário próprio e permitem praticar desde o início a compreensão da leitura.

TAKE-AWAY ENGLISH | Inclui expressões, frases feitas e locuções, com seus equivalentes em português e recomendações de uso.

GLOSSARY | Nesta parte você vai encontrar, em ordem alfabética e com tradução para o português, as palavras novas que apareceram na seção.

TRANSCRIPT | A última parte inclui a transcrição completa da faixa.

CONTENTS

CD 1

TRACK 01 ▸▸ LET'S GET STARTED — 5
Grammar: **have got**, possessives and object pronouns | Vocabulary: family relations, greetings

TRACK 02 ▸▸ WHAT DO YOU DO? — 13
Grammar: the present simple, the auxiliary **do/does**, Wh- questions with and without **do**, the genitive | Vocabulary: verbs related to work, key expressions for politeness

TRACK 03 ▸▸ DREAM HOLIDAYS — 24
Grammar: **would like** + infinitive/noun, **me too** or **me neither** | Vocabulary: holidays and tourism, geographical terms, days of the week, months of the year

TRACK 04 ▸▸ NEW ZEALAND — 33
Grammar: the simple past, comparatives | Vocabulary: **stay** or **be**, phrasal verbs with **stay**, adjectives to describe places, people and food

TRACK 05 ▸▸ DENTAL HEALTH — 47
Grammar: **should** and **have to**, the -ing form (gerund) | Vocabulary: adverbs of frequency, manner and focusing

TRACK 06 ▸▸ RECIPE TIME — 52
Grammar: the imperative | Vocabulary: food lexis, cooking lexis

TRACK 07 ▸▸ ROB IN THE UK — 61
Grammar: the simple past | Vocabulary: **do** or **make**, **see** or **watch**, UK and US english

TRACK 08 ▸▸ THE OLYMPIC GAMES — 69
Grammar: the present perfect, the passive voice | Vocabulary: sports

TRACK 09 ▸▸ HOROSCOPES — 78
Grammar: the future | Vocabulary: dependent prepositions, adjectives for personality, adverbs of manner

TRACK 10 ▸▸ QUIZ SHOW — 87
Grammar: superlatives, **what** or **which** | Vocabulary: ordinal numbers

TRACK 11 ▸▸ THE SOUL OF A MAN — 94
Grammar: noun formation, question tags, past passive, **might** | Vocabulary: the preposition **like**

TRACK 12 ▸▸ SELLING PHONE IN — 103
Grammar: the present continuous | Vocabulary: **buy** and **sell**, **back**

CD 2

TRACK 01 ▸▸ LOVE AND MARRIAGE — 111
Grammar: **have (got) to** + infinitive | Vocabulary: **get**, wedding lexis

TRACK 02 ▸▸ FIRST LOVE — 117
Grammar: the past continuous, **shall I/we**, **had to** | Vocabulary: vocabulary to talk about love and relationships

TRACK 03 ▸▸ TEENAGERS & PARENTS — 126
Grammar: adverbs of frequency, **let** | Vocabulary: phrasal verbs

TRACK 04 ▸▸ PETER LOVEDAY — 131
Grammar: past simple vs. present perfect, irregular past participles, present perfect continuous | Vocabulary: **fun** or **funny**, **play**, **get on (with)**, music lexis

TRACK 05 ▸▸ FASHION — 141
Grammar: future continuous, **be going to** + infinitive | Vocabulary: colours, clothes, materials, UK and US English

TRACKS 06-10 ▸▸ LANGUAGE COMMENTARY — 149

ANSWER KEY — 154

TRACK 01 / CD 1 ▶▶ **LET'S GET STARTED**

LISTENING

1 Escute e coloque os temas em ordem de aparição. Escreva o número.

- [1] your job
- [ ] sport
- [ ] food
- [ ] holidays
- [ ] quiz
- [ ] selling phone-in
- [ ] recent holidays
- [ ] music
- [ ] teenagers
- [ ] life in different places
- [ ] interview with dental hygienist
- [ ] weddings
- [ ] horoscopes

2 Marque a opção correta. Em um caso há 4 opções corretas.

1. The Horoscopes part is for...
   - a) today
   - b) tomorrow
   - c) next week
   - d) next month
   - e) next year

2. The quiz is about...
   - a) art
   - b) geography
   - c) history
   - d) science
   - e) sport

3. The teenagers are talking about...
   - a) love
   - b) music
   - c) sex
   - d) technology
   - e) their parents

4. People phone the show because there are things they want to...
   - a) borrow
   - b) buy
   - c) find
   - d) give away
   - e) sell

5. The final part is about...
   - a) finding a partner
   - b) locations
   - c) marriage
   - d) organisation of weddings
   - e) relationships

3 Busque as perguntas abaixo na gravação. Que palavra de cada sentença é pronunciada com mais ênfase? Marque-a. A entonação é ascendente ou descendente? Em seguida, repita cada uma, tentando imitar a pronúncia e a entonação.

How are you today, Stuart? Is that the same as a dentist?
And what's that about? And what's the quiz about?
And then? With your parents or your children?
Your favourite food? So is that it for today?

VOCABULARY

Family relations

4 Coloque os nomes de relações de parentesco indicados no quadro abaixo na coluna correta.

> wife · children · sister · husband · parents · brother · boyfriend · partner
> mother · father · girlfriend · son · daughter

Feminine	Feminine or masculine	Masculine

Atenção! Em inglês, **sons** ("filhos") é usado somente para meninos. Para nos referirmos tanto a filhos quanto a filhas, temos de dizer **sons and daughters** ou **children**. É por esta razão que em inglês não existe a palavra *fathers (porque só se tem um pai).

5 Faça o mesmo com as relações de parentesco indicadas abaixo.

> cousin · grandchildren · uncle · nephew · grandmother · aunt · grandparents
> niece · grandfather · granddaughter · grandson

Feminine	Feminine or masculine	Masculine

Atenção! Em inglês, **grandsons** ("netos") é usado somente para meninos. Para nos referirmos tanto a netos quanto a netas, temos de dizer **grandsons and granddaughters** ou **grandchildren**. A palavra **grandfathers** designa somente o pai do pai e o pai da mãe.

6 Relacione os termos.

> girlfriend · son · sister · daughter · uncle · children · aunt · grandchildren

1. Wife with **husband**
2. Mother/father with ...., ... and ....
3. Brother with ....
4. Boyfriend with ....
5. Nephew/niece with .... and ....
6. Grandparents with ....

People

A palavra **people** ("gente") é plural. Não seria dito, por exemplo, **Ten people is waiting for you, Dr. Sikorski**, mas sim **Ten people are waiting for you, Dr. Sikorski**.

Advice

A palavra **advice** ("conselho") é incontável. Nunca vem acompanhada de artigo indefinido: **I want to give you ~~an~~ advice.** / **Please don't ask me for advice.** / **Can I give you some advice?**

Greetings

No início da faixa, Stuart diz **Good morning, good afternoon or good evening, wherever you are**. Em inglês, diz-se **Good morning** até o meio-dia (midday). Após as 12h, diz-se **Good afternoon**. **The afternoon** vai das 12h até as 18h. A partir daí, diz-se **Good evening**. Depois das 18h, nas despedidas, dizemos **Goodbye** ou **Good night**.

Todas essas expressões servem tanto para saudar como para se despedir (exceto **Good night**, que é usado somente para se despedir). Equivalem a **Hello** e a **Goodbye**. **Bye** (pronunciado *bai*) e **bye bye** são abreviações de **Goodbye**. **Goodbye** vem da expressão God bide with thee (literalmente "Que Deus esteja com você!"), em inglês antigo. Na Austrália e na Nova Zelândia, diz-se **Gidday (Good-day)** para **Hello** e **Goodbye** a qualquer hora do dia.

GRAMMAR

Have got

O verbo **have got** equivale a "ter" em português.

- What **have we got** today, Stuart?   *O que temos hoje, Stuart?*
- Well, **we've got** a lot of things.   *Bem, temos muitas coisas.*

singular		plural	
I	have / 've (got)	We	have / 've (got)
You	have / 've (got)	You	have / 've (got)
He / she / it	has / 's (got)	They	have / 've (got)

A forma negativa é **haven't got** ou **hasn't got**.

We **haven't got** any children.
Robert **hasn't got** a mobile phone.

Não temos filhos.
Robert não tem celular.

Frequentemente se usa a forma mais curta (a segunda que aparece no quadro). Em inglês britânico, em situações formais, é comum usar **have** sem a forma **got**. Em inglês norte-americano, usa-se **have** para todos os tipos de situações.

7 Complete as frases abaixo com a forma correta de **have got**.

1. • We .... a small house on the coast.
   • Really? Are you rich?
   • No way – it's a really small house.

2. • How many children .... your brother .... ?
   • He .... five.
   • Five! That's incredible.

3. • .... your sister .... a boyfriend?
   • No, why?
   • Er, no special reason. But tell her that I .... a girlfriend, okay?

4. • Stuart .... a Canadian accent.
   • Ah, so he's not from the USA?
   • No, no, he's from Toronto.

5. • What a lot of CDs!
   • Yes, I think I .... more than 400.
   • But .... you .... time to listen to them?

6. • .... the USA .... 52 states?
   • I think so. But does that include Puerto Rico?
   • I really .... any idea.

7. • Can you help me with this Chemistry project?
   • Sorry, I can't do it today – I .... any time. Maybe tomorrow.
   • But tomorrow you .... a Physics exam.

8. • .... you .... a car?
   • Yes, it's a Ford Focus. What about you?
   • Yes, I .... a Renault Megane.

9. • What's your favourite national football team?
   • Well, Argentina .... normally .... a very good football team.
   • Yes, but they're not as good as Brazil in my opinion.

10. • Do you want to see some really old photos?
    • Okay. Oh, hey, look! Simon .... long hair in this one!
    • Oh yes, that one is at university, about 25 years ago.

Possessives and Object Pronouns

Preste atenção nestas duas frases que aparecem na faixa. As palavras que estão marcadas em negrito são adjetivos possessivos.

My name's Juliet and I'm **your** other co-host...
Talking about problems they have with **their** parents...

Assim como em português, os possessivos em inglês vêm antes dos substantivos.

My computer is very new.   *Meu computador é muito novo.*

Their university is close to where I live.   *A universidade deles está perto de onde eu moro.*

8 Complete a coluna do meio com os possessivos que faltam.

> my· their· her· our· his

Singular subject pronoun	Singular possessive	Singular object pronoun
I		me
you	your	you
he		
she		
it	its	it
Plural subject pronoun	Plural possessive	Plural object pronoun
we		
you	your	you
they		

Agora, preste atenção em outra frase que também aparece na gravação. A palavra marcada em negrito é um pronome objeto.

She's got some good advice for **us**.   *Ela tem um bom conselho para nós.*

Agora tente completar a terceira coluna com estes pronomes objetos. Na parte de soluções **(answer key)** você tem o quadro completo e traduzido para o português.

> us · them · her · him

Take-away English

Is that it?	*Isso é tudo?*
Keep listening.	*Continue escutando.*
Let's get started.	*Vamos começar.*
Right.	*Certo. / Ok.*
That sounds good.	*Parece bom.*
That's it.	*Pronto.*
What about you?	*E você?*
What's that about?	*Do que se trata?*

Glossary

a bit	um pouco	other	outro/a/os/as
about	sobre, a respeito de	parents	os pais
advice	conselho	partner (my)	companheiro/a (meu/minha)
already	já	people	gente
buy (to)	comprar	place	lugar
children	filhos, crianças	quite	bastante
co-host	coapresentador/ora	quiz	concurso
different	diferente	recent	recente
everyone	todo mundo	remember (to)	lembrar-se (de)
favourite	preferido/a	science	ciência
food	comida	see (to)	ver
geography	geografia	sell (to)	vender
guess (to)	adivinhar	sex	sexo
history	história	something	algo
holidays	férias	sport	esporte
host	apresentador/ora	teenager	adolescente
husband	marido/esposo	talk (to)	falar
interesting	interessante	today	hoje
interview	entrevista	try (to)	tentar
job	trabalho	unusual	incomum, insólito
join (to)	reunir-se, juntar-se	wait (to)	esperar
knowledge	conhecimento	wedding	casamento
life	vida	wife	mulher/esposa

Transcript

Stuart: Good morning, good afternoon or good evening, wherever you are. My name's Stuart Lewis and I'm your co-host today.

Juliet: And my name's Juliet Allen, and I'm your other co-host. How are you today, Stuart?

S: Fine, thanks. What about you, Juliet? How are you today?

J: Not bad, not bad at all. Now, thank you all for joining us. What have we got today, Stuart?

S: Well, Juliet, we've got a lot of things today in the show. First of all we've got *Tell us about your job* –

J: And what's that about?

S: Well, people phone in and tell us about interesting or unusual jobs that they have got.

J: That sounds good. And then?

S: And then we've got people talking about holidays that they'd like to have, then people talking about their recent holidays –

J: And after that we've got people talking about life in different places, then something about your favourite food.

S: Your favourite food? Hmm, good. Right, after that we've got an interview with a dental hygienist –

J: A dental hygienist? Is that the same as a dentist?

S: Oh no it isn't. It's quite different. Just wait and see.

J: What have we got after that? Well, we've got something about music, and then something about great moments in sport, and then your horoscopes for the next week, then a quiz –

S: And what's the quiz about?

J: It's a general knowledge quiz – geography, science, history, sport – a bit of everything. And that's not everything for today, because then we've got two teenagers talking about – let me guess – music? Love? Sex? Technology?

S: No, talking about problems they have with their parents.

J: Oh yes, I remember that!

S: With your parents or your children?

J: Both – with my parents *and* my children. So is that it for today?

S: Oh no. Then we've got people phoning in and trying to sell things, so if you want to buy something, keep listening. And finally, we've got someone talking about organising weddings –

J: About finding a partner – a wife or a husband, you mean?

S: No, she's talking about organising the wedding if you've already got a partner, and she's got some good advice for us, I think.

J: Okay, so let's get started!

TRACK 02 / CD 1 ▶▶ WHAT DO YOU DO?

LISTENING

1 Coloque as palavras na ordem correta para formar a pergunta "O que o Dean faz?".

Dean's / what / job / is / ?

2 Agora, marque a alternativa correta em cada caso.

1. Dean
   - a) exports meat to Australia.
   - b) imports meat from Australia and New Zealand.
   - c) imports animals from Australia.
   - d) imports animals from Australia and meat from New Zealand.

2. His customers are
   - a) hotels and restaurants.
   - b) catering companies and hotels.
   - c) large supermarkets.
   - d) butchers.

3. Dean travels to see his clients
   - a) very often.
   - b) often.
   - c) not much.
   - d) never.

4. Dean is happy in his job because
   - a) restaurant and hotel clients have a professional attitude.
   - b) restaurant and hotel clients appreciate good food.
   - c) restaurant and hotel chefs are very good customers.
   - d) restaurant and hotel chefs are real professionals.

3 Agora, coloque as palavras na ordem correta para formar a pergunta "O que a Tunde faz?". Note que se usa uma construção diferente da de Dean.

Tunde / does / what / do / ?

4 Agora, marque a opção correta em cada caso.

1. Tunde
   - a) publishes a magazine.
   - b) works in a hotel marketing department.
   - c) inspects hotels for a travel publication.
   - d) writes for *Vogue* and *GQ*.

2. In the hotels
   - a) nobody knows who she really is.
   - b) only one person knows who she really is.
   - c) the reception staff know who she really is.
   - d) the restaurant staff know who she really is.

3. She travels
   - a) to trade fairs in London.
   - b) to trade fairs and London.
   - c) by train to London.
   - d) by train and ferry to London.

4. Tunde's area is
   - a) Spain.
   - b) Andorra and Catalonia.
   - c) Andorra, the Balearic Islands and Catalonia.
   - d) Andalusia and Catalonia.

5 Relacione os tipos de carne com seu equivalente em português.

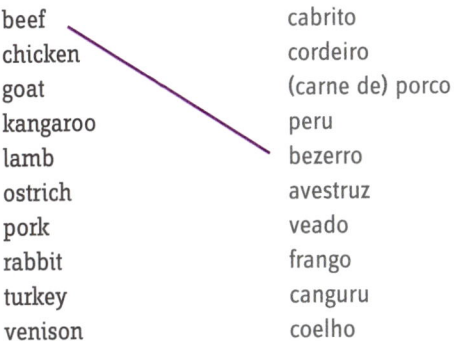

beef	cabrito
chicken	cordeiro
goat	(carne de) porco
kangaroo	peru
lamb	bezerro
ostrich	avestruz
pork	veado
rabbit	frango
turkey	canguru
venison	coelho

6 Que tipos de carne o Dean comercializa?

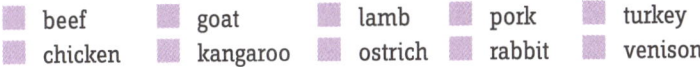

☐ beef ☐ goat ☐ lamb ☐ pork ☐ turkey
☐ chicken ☐ kangaroo ☐ ostrich ☐ rabbit ☐ venison

7 Marque se as frases sobre a Tunde são verdadeiras ou falsas.

	true	false
1. Hotels contact her because they want to be in the guide that she works for.		
2. Some of the hotels she visits are already in the guide.		
3. For her work, it's important that hotel staff think she is a normal guest.		
4. In the past, her area of work was smaller then it is now.		
5. She likes most of the people who work in the hotel industry.		

8 Escute este fragmento e marque as palavras que a Tunde enfatiza. Depois, repita-as em voz alta, imitando a pronúncia.

Well, first I check the websites of the new hotels I want to visit in a certain area, and then I call them to make an appointment. Next, I follow that up with an email and I also email all our participating hotels in that area to make appointments with them, too.

GRAMMAR

The present simple

9 Marque a pessoa em que estes verbos estão conjugados.

singular				plural		
1st pers.	2nd pers.	3rd pers.		1st pers.	2nd pers.	3rd pers.
			I **work** for a hotel guide.			
			... the guide **is** very exclusive.			
			... and the standards **are** very high.			
			They **are** part of the Condé Nast group			
			... what they **offer** to the clients.			
			I'm sure you **know** *Vogue* and *GQ*.			
			... how they **want** to market the hotel.			
			My contact **does**, of course.			
			The hotel industry **attracts** sociable people.			
			She **travels** around Spain inspecting hotels.			

10 Marque a opção correta de acordo com o caso.

No **present simple**, a única mudança verbal ocorre nas **primeira / segunda / terceira** pessoas do **singular / plural** da afirmativa, nas quais se acrescenta **-ed / -s / -is** à raiz do verbo.

11 Sublinhe (**underline**) a forma correta em cada caso.

Simon **come / comes** from Cambridge, in Britain, but he **live / lives** in Saudi Arabia. He **teach / teaches** English there, and he **work / works** for a large British company. He **drive / drives** to and from work and it **take / takes** him about 20 minutes. He **work / works** from 06.30 until 12.00 every day, and in the afternoon he **prepare / prepares** his classes and **study / studies** for his Master's degree. Because he **start / starts** work very early, he **go / goes** to bed at about 10.30.

Usamos o **present simple** para falar de:
- hábitos ou rotina: **We have paella every Sunday**.
- horários: **This train stops at Guadalajara**.
- coisas que são verdade hoje, mas podem deixar de ser: **We live in London**.
- afirmações atemporais: **Lisbon is the capital of Portugal**.
- leis científicas etc.: **Water boils at 100° Centigrade**.
- coisas que certamente vão acontecer no futuro: **The Tour of France begins this weekend**.

The auxiliary do/does

12 Estas perguntas aparecem nas entrevistas. Separe-as em dois grupos: perguntas fechadas (que exigem a resposta "sim" ou "não") ou perguntas abertas (a resposta é uma informação concreta ou uma explicação).

Do you travel much in your job?   Do they give you special treatment?
Who do you sell to?   What do you mean?
Who do you work for?   Do you like your job?
What does your work involve?   Do you ever get tired of travelling?

1) Yes / No questions	2) Information / Explanation answer

Agora, tente responder às perguntas abaixo.

Yes / No questions:
What is the first word? ....
What type of word is the second word? ....
What form is the main verb? ....

Perguntas como essas podem começar também com outros verbos auxiliares.

Can you tell us about your daily routine?   *Você pode nos contar sobre sua rotina diária?*

Could you tell us about your job?   *Você poderia nos contar sobre seu trabalho?*

Information / Explanation answer:
What type of word is the first word? ....
What type of word is the second word? ....
What form is the main verb? ....

Nesse tipo de pergunta, conhecemos o assunto da resposta e o verbo principal, mas não o objeto. Costumam começar com interrogativos, como **where** ("onde"), **why** ("por que"), **when** ("quando") ou **which** ("que", "qual/quais").

13 Organize as palavras para formar as perguntas.

1. the / play / where / children / do / ?
2. that / girl / who / is / ?
3. smoke / do / you / ?
4. Tupy / can / speak / she / ?
5. happen / does / why / this / ?
6. live / you / where / do / ?
7. Salvador Dalí / do / you / like / ?
8. sister / football / your / play / does / ?
9. Recife / from / do / you / come / ?

The genitive

Dean's job significa "o trabalho de Dean". Usamos esta forma **(the genitive)** para nos referirmos a coisas ou a qualidades que pertencem ou fazem parte de uma pessoa ou animal ou de um grupo de pessoas ou animais. Veja estes exemplos:

the King**'s** skis	os esquis do Rei
my parent**s'** generation	a geração de meus pais
sheep**'s** milk	leite de ovelha
Martha**'s** husband	o marido de Martha
Tom**'s** bike	a bicicleta de Tom
the party**'s** decision	a decisão do partido (político)
a children**'s** party	uma festa de criança
the cat**'s** food	a comida do gato
the team**'s** performance	a atuação do time

O genitivo também é usado com expressões de tempo, distância etc.

today's news	as notícias de hoje
tomorrow's match	o jogo de amanhã
next month's election	os comícios do mês que vem
yesterday's papers	os jornais de ontem
a mile's walk	uma caminhada de 1 km

Atenção! A posição do apóstrofo é importante. Veja a diferença entre as duas frases abaixo:

my bother's toys	os brinquedos do meu irmão
my brothers' toys	os brinquedos de meus irmãos

VOCABULARY

14 Estes verbos foram usados nos diálogos para falar de trabalho. Escreva a tradução. Pode consultar um glossário ou um dicionário.

arrange	get tired of
book	import
call	make an appointment
develop	market
enjoy	publish
find out	take something seriously
follow up	travel

15 Agora, tente responder a cada uma das perguntas:

In your work, what or who do you...
- arrange?
- call?
- enjoy?
- find out?
- follow up?
- get tired of?
- take seriously?

In your work, do you...
- book anything?
- develop anything?
- make appointments?
- import anything?
- market anything?
- publish anything?
- travel?

Take-away English

O conceito de **politeness** ("educação") na linguagem falada é importante em inglês. Em geral, as pessoas costumam ser menos diretas do que no Brasil. Vejamos algumas expressões que aparecem na faixa:

Excuse me, sir/madam
É usado para chamar a atenção ou para pedir passagem.

Pleased to meet you
É usado para saudar em situações formais. A resposta é **Pleased to meet you**. Uma opção é **How do you do**. Em situações informais, usa-se **Hello** ou **Hi**.

Please significa "por favor"; é pouco polite não usá-lo quando você pede algo. É colocado antes do verbo: **Please wait here**; ou no final da frase: **Could I speak to you, please?**

If you don't mind
Serve para pedir licença em situações mais ou menos formais ("se você não se importa").

Thank you very much
É usado para agradecer. De acordo com a situação, pode-se dizer **Thanks very much, Thanks a lot, Thank you** ou **Thanks**.

You're welcome / Not at all
São formas de dizer "de nada". Antigamente **You're welcome** era norte-americano e **Not at all**, britânico, mas hoje em dia se usa mais **You're welcome** em todos os lugares.

CULTURAL note

In English often the names of animals and the word for meat from those animals is different, for example the meat is **pork** but the animal is **pig**, the meat is **mutton** but the animal is **sheep**, the meat is **beef** or **veal** but the animal is **cow**. Why is this? In 1066 Anglo-Saxon England was conquered by the Normans, and for three centuries the upper-classes spoke French. They used French words for meat, like **mutton, pork, beef** and **veal** at the table, but they had no contact with living animals on farms. The Anglo-Saxon lower classes working in agriculture did have contact with living animals and continued to use the old English names, like **pig, sheep** or **cow**. This distinction became cemented in the English language.

Glossary

beef: carne de boi	carne de carneiro	de porco
cow: vaca	**pig**: porco	**sheep**: ovelha
mutton:	**pork**: carne	**veal**: carne de vitela

Glossary

a few	alguns/algumas	arrive (to)	chegar
airport	aeroporto	ask (to)	perguntar/pedir
all over	por todos os lados	attract (to)	atrair
amazing	incrível	beautiful	charmoso(a)/bonito(a)
amount	quantidade	beef	carne de boi
appointment	encontro/entrevista	big	grande
arrange (to)	organizar, arrumar	book (to)	reservar

call (to)	ligar (telefone)
car hire	aluguel de carros
chambermaid	camareira (de quarto de hotel)
check (to)	verificar, checar
client	cliente
company	empresa
confess (to)	admitir
cover (to)	cobrir
cuisine	a cozinha, culinária típica
daily	diariamente, cotidiano
delivery	entrega
deer	veado
destination	destino
develop (to)	desenvolver
director	gerente, diretor/a
disappointed	decepcionado/a
dislike (to)	não gostar
eat (to)	comer
enjoy (to)	desfrutar
enormous	enorme
enough	bastante, suficiente
explain (to)	explicar
ever	alguma vez
fat	gordura, gordo
find out (to)	descobrir, saber
flat	apartamento
friend	amigo/a
follow up (to)	seguir
food	comida
get tired of	cansar-se de
go (to)	ir
great	extraordinário/a
grow (to)	crescer
guest	cliente, hóspede
guide	guia
head office (UK)	sede (de uma empresa)
headquarters (US)	sede (de uma empresa)
help (to)	ajudar
high	alto/a (para casas)
import (to)	importar
involve (to)	incluir, envolver
job	emprego, trabalho
just	apenas/somente
know (to)	conhecer, saber
large	grande
logistics	logística
lovely	magnífico/a
low	baixo/a
magazine	revista
market (to)	comercializar
maybe	talvez
meat	carne
minute	minuto
more often	com mais frequência
never	nunca
of course	claro que sim
offer (to)	oferecer
once	uma vez
owner	proprietário/a
part of	parte de
pleasure	prazer
porter	porteiro/a
prefer (to)	preferir
protein	proteína
publish (to)	publicar
quick	rápido/a
reader	leitor
routine	rotina
seriously	sério
staff	equipe, trabalhadores
standard	nível, qualidade
stay (to)	ficar, permanecer
street	rua
take seriously	levar a sério
too much	demais
trade fair	feira de negócios
travel (to)	viajar
treatment	tratamento
typical	típico/a
usually	normalmente, em geral
venison	carne de veado
waiter	garçom
walk (to)	caminhar, passear
weekly	semanal
which	o qual, que, quais
work	trabalho
within	dentro de

Transcript

1

Brian: Welcome to *What do you do?* In which we ask people in the street about their jobs and their daily routines. Excuse me, sir, have you got a few minutes?

Dean: Ah, yes, if it's quick.

B: First of all, what's your name?

D: Dean Malcolm, my name's Dean Malcolm.

B: And my name's Brian. Pleased to meet you, Dean. Now, what do you do, Dean?

D: My job? Well, I'm a company owner and director.

B: And if you don't mind, could you tell us a bit about your job?

D: Not at all, I import meat products from Australia and New Zealand.

B: Really?

D: Yes, kangaroo from Australia, and lamb, beef and venison from New Zealand.

B: Venison?

D: Yes, deer meat.

B: Wow. And kangaroo?

D: Yes, it's a very high protein, low fat meat.

B: That's very interesting – and who do you sell to?

D: Mainly I sell to restaurants and hotels.

B: Can you tell us about your daily or weekly routine?

D: My day consists of arranging logistics for deliveries of products to clients. Also contacting and developing new clients.

B: Dean, do you travel much in your job?

D: I travel sometimes but not very much because so much of my work is done by telephone and by email.

B: Is there anything that you especially like or dislike about your job?

D: I enjoy my job a lot because cuisine is a very important industry, and the chefs of restaurants and hotels are real professionals who take their work very seriously and work with a lot of pleasure in what they offer to their clients.

B: Dean, thank you very much.

D: You're welcome.

2

Brian: Er – Excuse me, madam, have you got a few minutes?

Tunde: Yes, okay.

B: Yes of course. First of all, what's your name?

T: Tunde Longmore. Call me Tunde.

B: Hello Tunde, I'm Brian Brennan. Pleased to meet you. Tunde, what's your job?

T: I'm a hotel inspector.

B: And who do you work for?

T: I work for a hotel guide called Condé Nast Johansens. They are part of the Condé Nast group who publish *Vogue* and *GQ* – I'm sure you know *Vogue* and *GQ* – and lots of other magazines too.

B: And what does your work involve then?

T: Well, it involves visiting and selecting hotels that are good enough to go in the guide.

B: Really?

T: Yes, the guide is very exclusive and the standards are very high, so that our readers are never disappointed. So I have to walk around the hotel and try the restaurant, and see all the installations, and talk to the owner or the commercial director, to find out who their guests are, and how they want to market the hotel.

B: Wow. That sounds great! Is it?

T: Yes, I love my job and I've seen lots of amazing hotels

B: And do they give you special treatment?

T: Well, usually they don't, because not everyone knows who I am. My contact does, of course, but in a large hotel I can come in contact with the reception, the porters, the waiters the chambermaids, the spa staff and lots more people, who don't have any idea that I'm more than a normal guest, so I see how all the guests are treated, which is how it should be of course.

B: So what would be a typical week for you?

T: Well, first I check the websites of the new hotels I want to visit in a certain area, and then I call to make an appointment. Next, I follow that up with an email and I also email all our participating hotels in that area to make appointments with them, too.

B: Sorry Tunde – when you say participating hotels, what do you mean?

T: Hotels that are already in the guide. After that, I have to book the flight or phone the car hire company. And once I arrive at my destination I go from hotel to hotel to make my selection, and finally explain to them how we help them to market their property. And then I go home and write my reports.

B: So you travel a lot in your job, don't you?

T: Yes, I have to travel an enormous amount, not only to the hotels, but to trade fairs, to London, where our head office is. I used to cover all of Spain and the Spanish Islands, but we've grown so big that I just have Catalonia, Andorra and the Balearics now.

B: Do you like your job?

T: I love it! I love travelling and seeing so much of Spain, which is a beautiful, diverse country, and I love staying in lovely hotels and eating good food.

B: Do you ever get tired of travelling?

T: Yes, sometimes. I have to confess that sometimes I would prefer to be in my own home and of course, see my friends more often.

B: Of course, yes. Finally Tunde, can you tell us what you like and/or dislike about your job?

T: Right, I like the travelling – most of the time – and the people I work with and the people I come in contact with. The hotel industry attracts sociable, generous people. I also get great interior décor ideas for my flat. There is very little I dislike, except maybe too much time at airports.

B: Well, thank you very much, Tunde.

T: Not at all, Brian.

B: That was Tunde. She travels around Spain inspecting hotels for a travel publication in the UK.

TRACK 03 / CD 1 ▶▶ DREAM HOLIDAYS

LISTENING

1 Escreva o(os) destino(s) sonhado(s) de cada um. Atenção! Há três lugares que não são mencionados.

India · Sri Lanka · Nepal · The Seychelles · The Maldives · Colombia · Costa Rica

Sue: _____ Juliet: _____ Stuart: _____

2 Quais são as razões? Complete o quadro.

Sue · Juliet · Stuart · Nobody

1. Because it's good for walking.
2. Because it's culturally interesting.
3. Because it's typical.
4. Because it's tropical.
5. Because it's beautiful.
6. Because it's not too expensive.
7. Because of the silence.
8. Because of the peace.
9. Because of the beaches.
10. Because it's a paradise for vegetarians.
11. Because it's a paradise for vegetation.

3 Escute a frase **I want to talk about holidays** e a repita imitando a pronúncia. Quais são as três sílabas que são pronunciadas com maior ênfase? Em seguida, observe como é pronunciado **want to talk**.

Escute **I love holidays, when I can get them**. Quais são as duas palavras que são pronunciadas com maior ênfase? Em seguida, observe como é pronunciado **can get them**.

Agora, observe a frase **But I think that's the same for everyone**. Quais são as três sílabas que são pronunciadas com maior ênfase? Em seguida, observe como é pronunciado **for everyone**.

Por último, observe a frase **Now I want to ask you both a question about holidays**. Quais são as três sílabas que são pronunciadas com maior ênfase? Em seguida, observe como é pronunciado **want to ask you**.

VOCABULARY

Holidays and tourism

4 Estas palavras aparecem na faixa. Coloque-as em seu lugar correspondente.

> beach · destination · dream · holiday · island · mountain · peace · place silence · tourism · vegetation · water **/** beautiful · clean · cultural dependent on · exclusive · expensive · interesting **/** walk · swim

nouns		adjectives	
	sonho, ideal		cultural
	montanha		exclusivo
	paz		maravilhoso
	praia		caro
	turismo		limpo
	destino, lugar		interessante
	férias		que vive de
	flora, vegetação		
	ilha		verbs
	água		caminhar
	silêncio		nadar
	lugar		

5 Complete os textos com as palavras que faltam.

> tourism · beach · dependent · clean · swim · islands · destinations · holidays · beautiful

One of the most important industries in Spain is ▆▆▆▆▆▆▆ but the Balearic and Canary ▆▆▆▆▆▆▆ are now so exploited for summer

_____ that sometimes it isn't easy to find space for your towel on the _____. Apart from the islands, the main tourist _____ are the Costa Brava and Andalusia. Many villages that were once small and _____ are now large, ugly towns completely _____ on tourism. The sea often isn't _____, and because of climate change, warm-water sea creatures can make it dangerous for people who are trying to _____.

> mountains · walk · cultural · silence

In contrast, rural and _____ tourism are less developed in Spain, and in the _____ there is still _____ and there are wonderful places to _____.

> water · expensive · nature · place · vegetation · exclusive

On the coast and inland, local councils sell land to build thousands of _____ new houses for northern Europeans who are looking for a _____ in the sun, and _____ golf courses that require a tremendous amount of _____, in areas that have very little rain. In this process, as ecologists say, the first thing to be destroyed is the _____ and that has a negative impact on all the others elements of _____ like birds, animals and insects.

Geographical terms

6 Observe as palavras marcadas em negrito. São os pontos cardeais. Coloque-os (junto aos demais: **north**, **east**) em seu devido lugar.

The Maldives are just **south** of India and to the **west** of Sri Lanka.

7 Relacione as frases da esquerda com seu correspondente da direita.

1. Where's Belém?
2. We go ski-ing in Font Romeu.
3. I come from Vancouver.
4. Do you know Besançon?
5. Where do you go on holiday?
6. Where's Cuaibá?
7. Is Patagonia in Argentina or Chile?
8. Where are your family from?
9. Where's Newcastle-on-Tyne?

a) Usually we go to Bombinhas, on the south coast of Brazil.
b) It's in the south of Argentina.
c) Isn't that in the south of France?
d) It's in the west of Brazil.
e) I do, actually. It's in the east of France.
f) It's in the north east of England.
g) That's in the west of Canada, isn't it?
h) In the north of Brazil.
i) We're from Galway, on the west coast of Ireland.

O adjetivo é formado com o ponto cardeal (**north**, **south**, **east**, **west**) + a terminação **-ern**: **northern**, **southern**, **eastern**, **western**. Dois exemplos: **The Industrial Revolution began in Northern England** ("A Revolução Industrial começou no norte da Inglaterra); **"Western people will never understand us", he said** ("Os ocidentais nunca nos entenderão", disse). Atenção! Dizemos **in** the north/south/east/west, mas **on** the west coast: **We live on the West Coast, in southern California.**

Days of the week and months of the year

8 Coloque as palavras no lugar e na ordem correta.

April · Sunday · September · Saturday · August · December · February
Friday · June · Tuesday · November · January · Monday · Thursday
October · March · July · Wednesday · May

	Days of the week		Months
1		1	
2		2	
3		3	
4		4	**April**
5		5	

6		6	
7	**Sunday**	7	
		8	
		9	
		10	
		11	
		12	

9 Leia o texto sobre os nomes dos dias da semana e responda às perguntas.

England was colonised by Norsemen (also called *Danes* or *Vikings*) in the 10th century. The origin of six of the days in English comes from the pagan Germanic and Norse mythology, and one comes directly from Latin.

- How do you say *sol* in English? _____ Which day of the week does it correspond to? _____ Traditionally, this is the first day of the week, but nowadays for most people it is the last day. In Latin it was *dies solis*.
- How do you say *lua* in English? _____ Which day of the week does it correspond to? _____
- In Norse mythology *Tiw* was the god of war. Which Roman god does he correspond to? _____ In English his day is called _____
- Germanic mythology calls him *Wotan* and the Vikings called him *Odin*. He corresponds to Mercury in Roman mythology. The capital city of Scotland is named after him. In modern English this day is called what? _____
- In Norse mythology *Thor* was the king of the gods. In Roman mythology the correspondent god was called *Jupiter*. Which day is his in English? _____
- In Germanic mythology *Frig* (or *Fria*) was the goddess of love and sex. Which Roman goddess does she correspond to? _____ Which day is named after her in English? _____
- Traditionally this is the last day of the week, and it is still the holy day in the Jewish religion. Its English name comes from the Roman god Saturn. It's _____

Vacation or holiday?

"Férias" em inglês americano é **vacation** e em inglês britânico, **holiday**. Antigamente os únicos dias livres da semana eram as festas religiosas, e o inglês britânico reflete essa origem: **holy** (sagrado) + **day**. Em todas as variantes do inglês, é usado **holiday** para se referir a um dia em que não se trabalha, como **thanksgiving** nos Estados Unidos ou **Saint Patricks' Day** na Irlanda. Atenção! Com **holiday** e **vacation** sempre se usa a preposição **on**: **Where are you going on holiday? / We're on vacation next week.**

This, last or next?

Last Friday é sexta-feira passada. **This Friday** é esta sexta-feira, a que pertence a esta semana. **Next Friday** é a sexta da semana que vem.

GRAMMAR

Would like + infinitive/noun

Quando Sue diz **I'd like to go to a small island** ela está se referindo a algo imaginário ou hipotético. A construção sujeito + **would** + **like** + infinitivo serve para: a) expressar um desejo pouco provável ou algo que não é possível agora; b) pedir algo de forma cortês; c) pedir a alguém, educadamente, que faça algo.

10 Leia as frases e marque se corresponde à opção a, b ou c mencionada anteriormente.

1. A lot of African people would like to live in Europe.
2. Would you like to wait here please?
3. I'd like to book a room for three nights, please.
4. I'd like to help you, but I can't.
5. We'd like to speak to the manager, please.
6. I'm sorry, Mrs Gore is in a meeting. Would you like to phone later?
7. Which famous person would you like to meet?
8. Would you like to marry me?

A construção sujeito + **would** + **like** + nome serve para: a) oferecer algo a alguém; b) pedir algo de forma educada.

11 Leia estas frases e marque a qual dos usos mencionados anteriormente (a ou b) se refere cada uma.

1. I'd like some information about sightseeing tours of the city.
2. Would you like some more wine?
3. Would they like pizza instead of pasta?
4. We'd like five tickets to see *Romeo and Juliet* on Friday 19th.
5. Would you like the vegetarian option?
6. Would you like something to eat?
7. I'd like an appointment to see Dr Patel today or tomorrow please.

Atenção! Literalmente **I would like** significa "eu gostaria", mas na verdade equivale mais a "eu quero", porque **I want** é muito direto e pouco cortês, principalmente no inglês britânico.

Me too or me neither

12 Procure na gravação as expressões **me too** e **me neither**. Qual significa "eu também" e qual significa "eu também não"? Em seguida, responda às frases abaixo com uma das duas opções.

1. I really don't like rap music.
2. I think Argentina will be the next world champions.
3. I think it's too hot in here.
4. My sister studies Physics at university.
5. Sorry, I don't understand that.
6. I can't speak German.
7. I think this place is beautiful.
8. I wouldn't like to be a vegetarian in this country.
9. I don't think I'd like to watch this film; it's really violent.
10. I'm not very happy with this situation.

Take-away English

How about you? e What about you? são formas muito comuns para solicitar uma resposta ou uma opinião sobre algo. Equivaleria aproximadamente a "O que você acha?".

I'm not so bad é uma forma frequente de dizer "Tudo bem" ou "Vou bem" quando alguém pergunta como estamos.

I mean...	Quero dizer...
It must be beautiful.	Deve ser maravilhoso...
Let's forget about...	Vamos nos esquecer de...
Oh great!	Perfeito! Genial!
We are joined by Sue.	A Sue vem com a gente.

Glossary

about	sobre, acerca de	join (to)	juntar-se, unir-se
active	ativo	last	mais recente / atual
anywhere	qualquer lugar	lie (to)	deitar-se
beach	praia	maybe	talvez
beautiful	maravilhoso	mountain	montanha
both	ambos(as)/os dois/ as duas	nature	natureza
		next	próximo/a
clean	limpo/a	other	outro/a
climb (to)	escalar	peace	paz
connect (to)	conectar	place	lugar
cultural	cultural	point of view	ponto de vista
dependent on	que vive de	real	real, verdadeiro
destination	destino, lugar	show	programa (de TV, rádio etc.)
dream	sonho, ideal		
especially	principalmente	silence	silêncio
exactly	exatamente	sky	céu
exclusive	exclusivo	somewhere	algum lugar
expensive	caro	south	sul
forget (to)	esquecer	swim (to)	nadar
God	Deus	vegetation	vegetação
Goddess	Deusa	the same	a mesma coisa
guys	caras (informal)	tourism	turismo
holiday	férias/feriado	walk (to)	caminhar
imagine (to)	imaginar	watch (to)	olhar
interesting	interessante	water	água
island	ilha		

Transcript

Stuart: And on with the show. Right now we're joined by Sue Bean. How are you, Sue?

Sue: I'm not so bad. How are you Stuart? Jules?

Stuart: Okay.

Juliet: Fine thanks.

S: Now you guys, listen to me – I want to talk about holidays. You know that, don't you?

J: Oh great, I love holidays, when I can get them.

St: Me too. But I think it's the same for everyone.

S: Now I want to ask you both a question about holidays.

St: About my last holiday?

S: No.

J: About our next holiday?

S: Well, no, not that either.

J: Well what then?

S: Okay, listen, where would like to go on holiday? I mean, if you could go anywhere in the world, where would it be? Where would you go?

St: Anywhere in the world? Anywhere at all?

J: I need a minute to think.

S: I know where I'd like to go.

J: Well, where would you go, Sue?

S: I'd like to go to a small island, somewhere tropical, the Seychelles – I'd love to go to the Seychelles. And the other place I'd love to go to is the Maldives.

J: Where exactly are the Maldives? I don't really know.

S: Me neither.

St: Aren't they in the Indian Ocean too? Just south of India and to the west of Sri Lanka.

S: Yeah, that's right. Those are the two places I'd like to go to. And maybe I will one day, who knows. What about you, Juliet?

J: Me, if I could go anywhere I think I'd like to go to Costa Rica.

S: Why Costa Rica?

J: Well, people say it's beautiful, a kind of paradise, at least for nature – you know – vegetation, animals, and beaches. And not too expensive or exclusive.

S: Okay, so that's Costa Rica for Juliet. And, how about you, Stuart?

St: It's not easy to say – there are so many places I'd like to go, but I think my dream destination would be Nepal.

S: Nepal? Why Nepal?

St: Because of the silence, the peace, the mountains, nature, clean air and water. I'd really like to go walking there. And I imagine it's not dependent on tourism.

J: Yes, I'd say that Nepal is probably more interesting from a cultural point of view than Costa Rica –

S: Or the Maldives or the Seychelles.

St: I think it must be beautiful to watch the sky at night in the mountains in a place like Nepal. Especially after a day of walking or climbing.

J: Well I think it must be equally beautiful to watch the sky at night in Costa Rica, especially after a day lying on the beach or swimming.

S: I think maybe Stuart is more active than we are. Okay, let's forget about dream holidays for a minute, because we're going to connect with Brian. He's talking to someone about a real holiday.

NEW ZEALAND

Part 1. *Karen's holiday*

LISTENING

1 Escute a primeira parte da faixa e marque no mapa os lugares que Karen menciona. Depois, marque em cada caso a opção correta.

1. Karen is talking about a holiday...
   - a) in the past
   - b) in the present
   - c) in the future

2. Karen was on holiday with her...
   - a) boyfriend
   - b) husband
   - c) family
   - d) parents

2 True or false?

	true	false
1. They were in New Zealand for three weeks.		
2. 75% of the New Zealand population live in Auckland.		
3. They didn't stay in hotels.		
4. They went to two football matches.		
5. Queenstown is a centre for high-risk activities.		
6. Somebody gave them free tickets to a rugby match.		
7. They had lunch in a Maori restaurant.		
8. A lot of the food there was new to Karen.		
9. Restaurants in New Zealand give bigger portions of food than in Europe.		

3 Complete o texto com os verbos abaixo.

> had · mentioned · drove · did · was · took

Well, we _____ down to Wellington and _____ the ferry to Picton, in the South island. Apart from the Kaikoura Coast, which I _____ before, maybe the best place _____ Queenstown – it's a town with a lot of extreme sports, I mean risk sports, like bungy-jumping, skiing, snowboarding, jet-boating, etc. We _____ some jet-boating and we _____ a really exciting morning.

GRAMMAR

4 Relacione as formas do passado com sua forma correspondente no presente.

> took · said · went · was / were · ate · could · had · saw

be ▶	**take** ▶	**say** ▶	**do** ▶ ....
can ▶	**see** ▶	**go** ▶	**have** ▶ ....

5 Escreva as formas do passado dos seguintes verbos em sua coluna correspondente: regulares ou irregulares. Se necessário, consulte o dicionário.

> like · rent · stay · want · drive · cook · put on · spend · impress · think

Regular	Irregular

6 Complete o resumo das férias de Karen com a forma no passado dos verbos entre parênteses.

Karen and her husband (**go**) .... on holiday to New Zealand. It (**take**) .... them 26 hours to fly there. They (**stay**) .... there for three weeks and (**travel**) .... around the country in a campervan. They (**not have**) .... a strict schedule, so if they (**like**) .... a place, they (**can**) .... spend more time there. While they (**be**) .... in New Zealand they (**see**) .... two rugby matches. Somebody (**give**) .... them free tickets for one of the matches because she said she (**not need**) .... them. Karen and her husband (**eat**) .... very well there, and both of them (**put on**) .... several kilos.

7 Tente responder às perguntas abaixo em seu caderno.

1. Procure na faixa dois verbos no passado na forma negativa, um com **was** e outro com **could**. Neste caso, o que você destaca?

2. Procure na faixa duas frases com um verbo no passado na forma negativa. Qual é a construção?

3. Procure três perguntas de respostas sim/não com **did**. Como são formadas?

4. Procure uma pergunta de resposta sim/não no passado **was/were**. Qual é a primeira palavra na oração interrogativa?

The simple past

No **simple past** os verbos têm uma única forma. Por exemplo, o verbo "ter".

singular		plural	
I	**had**	We	**had**
You	**had**	You	**had**
He / she / it	**had**	They	**had**

I **had** a small accident.   *Eu sofri um pequeno acidente.*
They **travelled** around the country.   *Eles viajaram por todo o país.*
I **went** to the cinema last night.   *Eu fui ao cinema ontem à noite.*

A única exceção é o verbo **to be** ("ser", "estar"), que tem duas formas: **was** e **were**.

singular		plural	
I	**was**	We	**were**
You	**were**	You	**were**
He / she / it	**was**	They	**were**

I **was** at home all day yesterday.   We **were** out when you phoned.

A negação é formada com **did** + **not** + infinitivo.

We **didn't see** the match.   I **didn't say** anything about you.

Se o verbo principal é um auxiliar, acrescentamos **not**.

I **wasn't** happy about changing to a new telephone company.
They **couldn't** arrive on time because of the traffic.

Para fazer uma pergunta de resposta sim/não no passado, usamos **did** + infinitivo.

Did she **accept** their offer of a new six-month contract?
Did the Minister of Defence **make** a comment about the tragedy?

Quando o verbo principal é um auxiliar, trocamos a ordem das palavras.

Were you at university in Bilbao too?
Could you really speak three languages when you were 12 years old?

VOCABULARY

8 Relacione as formas do passado com o equivalente de seu infinitivo em português.

> alugar · gastar · cozinhar · dirigir · pegar · engordar · hospedar-se · ir · querer · ver

cooked	drove	put on* ....
rented	spent	stayed* ....
took*	wanted	went ....
saw		*também têm outros significados

9 Relacione cada verbo com as palavras com que normalmente são usadas (**collocation**). Por exemplo: **ate + food**.

1	cooked	a	money / time
2	drove	b	food / dinner / lunch
3	put on	c	in a hotel / with friends
4	rented	d	a house / an apartment / a car
5	saw	e	a car / a bus
6	spent	f	a film / a match / a TV programme
7	stayed	g	photos / a ferry / a train
8	took	h	to the cinema / to work / out
9	wanted	i	two kilos
10	went	j	to rest / to do something / to go

10 Complete as frases seguintes com os verbos indicados no quadro em **simple past**.

> take · think · have · want · spend · like · can · stay · impress · give

1. Wolfgang Amadeus Mozart _____ play the piano when he five years old.
2. I _____ the people in Morocco a lot, but it was too hot for me.
3. The first time I heard him speak, the new president of the USA _____ me a lot.
4. When I was young, my parents usually _____ me money for my birthday.
5. Is it € 50? Sorry, I _____ you said € 15.
6. We _____ pasta and then lasagna for lunch at the new Italian restaurant.
7. The first time I was in Paris, I _____ 200 photos in three days.
8. I _____ so much money every day in London - even on basic things like public transport.
9. We _____ at a small family hotel for a week. It was great.
10. I'm really sorry - I _____ to phone you, but I didn't have any credit in my phone.

Stay

O verbo **stay** tem vários significados. Em alguns casos, equivale a "hospedar-se".

When we were in Prague we **stayed** with some friends in the old town.
Which hotel are you **staying** in?

Às vezes, equivale a "ficar", no sentido de permanecer.

Oh, won't you **stay**, just a little bit longer?
I'd like to **stay**, but I have to catch the last train.

Em outros, poderia ser traduzido como "continuar, seguir".

She **stayed** faithful to her husband, even after the accident.
The situation cannot **stay** like this.

11 Risque (**cross out**) o verbo não correspondente.

1. I **stayed** / **was** happy when I was at university.
2. Can I **stay** / **be** the night with you?
3. Why don't you **stay** / **be** for dinner?
4. We **stayed** / **were** very tired after the party.
5. I **stayed** / **was** trying to phone you all last week!
6. She's **staying** / **being** in a university residence not far from the new campus.
7. I'm in very good condition for my age and I want to **stay** / **be** healthy.
8. Mother's not well. Can you **stay** / **be** with her tonight?
9. Hello? Is that Human Resources? I **am** / **stay** trying to contact Mr Twide.
10. After a divorce, the children usually **stay** / **be** with their mother.

Phrasal verbs with stay

O verbo **stay** pode combinar com preposições para formar **phrasal verbs**.

stay in
Because of the horrible weather, we **stayed in** all weekend.
I'd love to go out tonight but I have to **stay in** and help my parents.

stay out
She's only 14 years old and she **stays out** until midnight.
Please **stay out** of this. This is a family question, and you are not family!

stay up
I **stayed up** all night finishing the project for my Economics class the next day.
Dad, please don't **stay up** for me; I'll be okay.

stay away
You **stay away** from my daughter or I'll kill you!
I think you should **stay away** from her, for you own sanity.

12 O que significa...? Escreva!

1. permanecer longe	
2. não se meter / não voltar para casa	
3. permanecer em casa	
4. não se deitar, ficar acordado	

13 Complete o texto com os verbos no **simple past**.

For our last holiday we _____ to the south of France. We _____ there for two weeks and it _____ absolutely wonderful. I _____ surprised at how cheap it is - much cheaper than Paris, for example, and we _____ a great time visiting the small towns and of course Sérgio _____ hundreds of photos on his new camera. We _____ some spectacular castles, which _____ part of the terrible story of what _____ to the Cathars. The food, of course, _____ superb, and I think we all _____ a few kilos. We _____ in small hotels and we _____ much less money than we _____ .

Take-away English

And apart from that?	E além disso? / E fora isso?
I'm mad about rugby.	Eu adoro rúgbi.
That was really interesting.	Foi muito interessante.
What impressed you the most?	O que mais te impressionou?

> **CULTURAL note**
>
> New Zealand consists of two islands – The North Island and The South Island. New Zealand is traditionally a **farming country** that **supplies** agricultural products and food, and **nowadays** the main **exports** are **dairy produce**, meat, **forestry products**, fruit, fish and wine. New Zealand makes some of the best white wines in the world. But it is **perhaps** more famous for its national rugby team – The All Blacks, and Peter Jackson's very **successful** trilogy of *The Lord of the Rings*, which was filmed entirely in New Zealand. People who visit the country are impressed by how green it is, and by the intense quality of the light.

Glossary

dairy produce: produtos lácteos	tor agrícola e de gado	**nowadays:** hoje em dia
exports: exportações	**forestry products:** indústria florestal	**perhaps:** talvez
farming country: país produ-	**impressed:** impressionado	**supply (to):** fornecer, prover

Part 2. Sue's comments

LISTENING

14 Escute a comparação que Sue faz da vida na Europa e na Nova Zelândia. Marque no quadro em qual dos lugares há mais de cada aspecto.

More in Western Europe		More in New Zealand
	high standard of living	
	high population density	
	tall buildings	
	big houses	
	wet weather	
	sunny weather	
	high price of food in supermarkets	
	high price of wine	
	high price of houses	
	independent people	
	family-focused people	

GRAMMAR

Comparatives

15 Quantas sílabas têm as palavras do quadro abaixo? Coloque-as na coluna correspondente.

> cheap · high · expensive · stupid · sexy · independent · sunny · thin · dry
> polite · big · happy · small · tall · complex · heavy · low · easy · difficult
> fat · populated · sweet · nice · fast · angry · beautiful · boring · hungry
> simple · helpful · slow · ugly · wet

One syllable	Two syllables (ending with -y)	Two syllables	Three or four syllables

16 Risque (**cross out**) as formas incorretas:

Sue says that the climate in New Zealand is **sunnier** / **more sunny** but also **wetter** / **more wet** than in most places in Western Europe. One of the main differences is that buildings in Europe are much **higher** / **more high**, but New Zealand houses are usually **bigger** / **more big**. Buying food in supermarkets is **less expensiver** / **less expensive** in NZ than where Sue lives in Europe, but because of tax, wine in New Zealand is **expensiver** / **more expensive**. When it comes to people, Sue says that a lot of New Zealanders are **fatter** / **more fat** than most Europeans, and they are also **independenter** / **more independent** than Europeans.

As formas comparativas do adjetivo seguem as seguintes regras:
a) Se o adjetivo é um monossílabo, acrescenta-se **-er** ao adjetivo seguido de **than**. Se terminar em consoante + vogal + consoante, dobra-se a última consoante.

b) Se o adjetivo tem duas sílabas e termina em **-y**, substituímos o **y** por **i**, acrescentamos **-er** à forma resultante e, em seguida, usamos **than**.

c) Se o adjetivo tem duas sílabas e NÃO termina em **-y**, colocamos **more** (+) or **less** (-) antes do adjetivo e **than** depois.

d) Se o adjetivo tem três ou mais sílabas, colocamos **more** (+) ou **less** (-) antes do adjetivo e **than** depois.

e) Há algumas exceções: **good** ▶ **better** (+ **than**), **bad** ▶ **worse** (+ **than**).

17 Agora, relacione cada exemplo com uma das regras apresentadas.

1. People say that Abrolhos is **more beautiful** than Ilha Grande.
2. They made the character **sexier** when they made the book into a film.
3. Why don't we buy this one? It's **cheaper**.
4. This question is **more complex** than you think.
5. Mmm... this wine is **better** that the first one we had.
6. The traffic was **worse** today than last Friday.

VOCABULARY

18 Coloque os adjetivos abaixo nos lugares corretos. Alguns podem se encaixar em mais de uma coluna.

> cheap · stupid · sexy · independent · sunny · thin · dry · polite · tall
> complex · heavy · easy · difficult · sweet · nice · beautiful · wet · short
> delicious · boring · simple · helpful · ugly · expensive

For a place	For a person: character	For a person: physical	For food

19 Olhe o quadro anterior e busque oito pares de sinônimos e antônimos.

ugly - beautiful	

20 Complete as frases com um dos adjetivos abaixo em sua forma comparativa. Atenção! Em uma frase, a comparação é de inferioridade (**less**).

> beautiful · cheap · difficult · dry · good · independent
> nice · sexy · sweet · simple

1. I hate that violent music! Why can't we listen to something a bit ....?
2. Lots of Norwegian people live in the northeast of Brazil for the climate and because it's .... than Norway.
3. Yes, these paintings by Renoir are less .... than some of his other work, but I love them.
4. My parents told me not to change my skirt, but I wanted to wear something .... for the party.
5. "How was the exam?" "Not good; it was .... than I thought."
6. "Do you feel as bad as you did yesterday?" "No, I feel a bit ...., thanks."
7. Americans usually like their chocolate to be .... than Europeans do.
8. You're making it too complicated – the question is much .... than that.
9. This wine is too sweet for me. Have you got something a little ....?
10. Mum, Dad, I don't need your help – I want to be ....

Take-away English

Anything else?	Algo mais?
generally speaking	em geral
I suppose (so).	Suponho.
more or less	mais ou menos
to be mad about something	ser fã de algo
What are the people like?	Como são as pessoas?

Glossary

Part 1

anywhere	qualquer lugar
bungy-jumping	praticar *bungee jump*
campervan	trailer
dinner	jantar
dolphin	golfinho
drive (to)	dirigir
exciting	demais, emocionante
fixed	fixo/a, preestabelecido/a
flight	voo
free	grátis
great	maravilhoso(a) / genial
hole	buraco
itself	em si mesmo (*pronome enfático*)
jet-boating	andar de *jet ski*
match	jogo, partida
middle	centro
mix	mistura
place	lugar
put on (to)	engordar
queue	fila
seal	foca
serving	porção (comida)
standard of living	padrão de vida
stone	pedra
stopover	escala (de voo)
there	lá
ticket	entrada, bilhete
trick	travessura, truque
underground	debaixo da terra
way	maneira, modo
whale	baleia

Part 2

away from	longe de
beer	cerveja
buy (to)	comprar
car	carro
eat out (to)	comer/jantar fora
family	família
in terms of	quanto a, referente a
in the sense	no sentido de
land	terra, terreno
lifestyle	estilo de vida
like	como, parecido com
mainly	principalmente
maybe	talvez
price	preço
rain	chuva
rain (to)	chover
similar to	parecido com / semelhante a
storey	andar (apartamento)
sunshine	sol, luz do sol
suppose (to)	supor
tax	impostos
wine	vinho

Transcript

Part 1

Brian: So, Karen, can you tell me about your last holiday?

Karen: Sure – it was a great holiday in fact. We went to New Zealand and we were there for three weeks. The flight took 26 hours, which was a very long flight for us, with two stopovers, in Paris and in Seoul. In New Zealand we rented a campervan so we could drive all over the country. We spent a week in the North Island and two weeks in the South Island.

B: What were the things that impressed you the most?

K: Well – the things that most impressed me were – er – mainly Auckland-

B: What impressed you about Auckland?

K: Well it's the biggest city in the country. Probably it's not very big in European terms, but 25% of the population of the country live there. It's got a high standard of living and it's an interesting mix of cultures. It's quite impressive.
B: And apart from Auckland?
K: The other thing that impressed me most was the Kaikoura Coast in the South Island. That was really interesting because we saw whales, seals and even dolphins. And another thing was the mountains of the South Island which are quite high, and are just in the middle of the island, so you have the sea on both sides. And-
B: Was it a good experience – travelling around in a campervan?
K: Yeah well, we – we, because I went there with my husband – we could go anywhere that we wanted. We didn't have a fixed schedule, so if we liked some place we could spend more time there, and if something well – you know – wasn't as interesting as we thought we could just continue driving.
B: Did you sleep in the campervan all the time?
K: No, not every night. We stayed with friends in Manukau and Dunedin.
B: Okay. Did you – How did you get to the South Island?
K: Well, we drove down to Wellington and took the ferry to Picton, in the South island. Apart from the Kaikoura Coast, which I mentioned before, maybe the best place was Queenstown – it's a town with a lot of extreme sports, I mean risk sports, like bungy-jumping, skiing, snowboarding, jet-boating, etc. We did some jet-boating and we had a really exciting morning. The town itself is quite small, but there's a lot of people all day round, lots of shops, and it's a very interesting place to go.
B: Did you do any kind of cultural activity?
K: Cultural? Well, we went to two rugby matches; you know my husband's mad about rugby. And when we were in the queue to get tickets someone came up to us and gave us free tickets.
B: Free tickets? How come?
K: She said that she didn't need them, because she had too many. We couldn't believe it! It was an important match. We thought – you know – it was a trick at first. But no, they were genuine tickets!
B: That was lucky, yeah. And do you like rugby?
K: Er – well, basically yes. Anyway, the match was Canterbury versus Auckland. It was a great match, really exciting.
B: So Karen, did you try any new kinds of food?
K: In Wellington we had dinner in a famous Maori restaurant called "Kai in the City" (Kai in Maori means food) and it was fine Maori cuisine, very curious because they prepare the meals in such a different way from the way we do. For instance, this food was cooked underground – in a hole in the ground, using hot stones.
B: Hmm. Anything else?
K: Well we ate some venison, and probably more than new food, the most interesting thing was eating probably the same things you eat here cooked in a different way, like

lamb or other kinds of meat cooked in different ways.
B: In general, how did you find the food?
K: Well – it was very good, I think the main thing was that they give you more food there in the restaurants than they do here – the servings in New Zealand are very generous. I think I put on three kilos and my husband put on four!
B: Thank you very much Karen. And now back to the studio.

Part 2

Juliet: Thanks, Brian. Now, Sue, you're from New Zealand, aren't you?
Sue: I certainly am.
J: And what do you think is different about New Zealand –
S: Compared to where?
J: To here, Western Europe.
S: I think the lifestyle is similar to Western Europe, generally speaking, but maybe New Zealand has a higher standard of living then some places in western Europe. But the main thing is that it's much less populated.
J: Fewer people?
S: Yes, I mean New Zealand is more or less the same size in terms of square kilometres as Britain or Italy, but there are only four million people there.
J: Really?
S: And buildings are much taller here. Most people in New Zealand live in bungalows, just one storey. With quite big gardens. People generally have bigger houses there.
J: So a house with two floors is quite unusual there?
S: Yeah. And the climate in the North Island is like the south of France or the north of Italy in terms of hours of sunshine and temperature, but it's a lot wetter – it rains a lot more. And in the south I suppose the temperatures are similar to the north of France or the north of Spain, but different in the sense that it's much sunnier.
J: What about prices?
S: Most things are quite similar to here, but supermarket food is maybe a bit cheaper there. I'd say that eating out in restaurants is also cheaper in New Zealand, but wine is more expensive, because of tax mainly.
J: Anything else?
S: Buying land or a house is less expensive in New Zealand than here, especially away from the big towns.
J: Interesting. Now, what about the people?
S: I think people in New Zealand are fatter – too much time in cars, and too much beer –
J: No, no, no, Sue –
S: Sorry, sorry, I shouldn't say *fat*, should I?
J: No, Sue, I mean what are the people like?
S: Oh, sorry. Right – er – I think people are more independent in New Zealand, less focused on their families maybe.
J: Thanks for that, Sue.

TRACK 05 / CD 1 ▶▶ DENTAL HEALTH

LISTENING

1 Responda às perguntas.

1. What do many people do badly? ....
....

2. How often should people see a dental hygienist? ....
....

3. What does she like about her work? ....
....

2 True or false? Marque.

	T	F
1. The job of a dental hygienist is to educate and motivate.		
2. Brushing often enough is not the most important thing.		
3. Dental plaque comes from saliva and food.		
4. Periodontal disease cannot be transmitted from one generation to another.		

3 Escute o final da faixa e sublinhe (**underline**) a palavra que você escutar.

I like seeing people, meeting people, discussing **things / thinks** with people. I create a whole scenario, because I like people for one thing, and I'm here to **help / educate** people, and that's really what it's all **for / about**.

4 Olhe a transcrição e procure as expressões que significam:

O mais importante	
O principal	
Nosso papel é	
Para começar	
Realmente é disso que se trata	

GRAMMAR

Should and have to

Usamos **should** para fazer recomendações. A estrutura é sempre:

> pronoun/subject + **should** + infinitive

Frases afirmativas: You **should** visit your aunt.
Frases negativas: You **shouldn't** smoke so much.
Perguntas: **Should** we tell Jonathan about this?
Perguntas negativas: **Shouldn't** you be here today?

Usamos **have to** para expressar obrigação. A estrutura é sempre:

> pronoun/subject + **have to** + infinitive

Frases afirmativas: You **have to** work harder.
Frases negativas: You **don't have to** eat it if you don't like it.
Perguntas: **Do I have to** take my passport if I go to France?

Atenção! Na terceira pessoa do singular, as formas são:

> he/she/it **has to**, he/she/it **doesn't have to**, **does** he/she/it **have to**

The -ing form (Gerund)

O gerúndio (**gerund** ou **-ing form**) é mais usado em inglês do que em português.

5 Relacione os exemplos seguintes com cada ponto da regra gramatical:

In English we use the gerund form:

a) after a preposition
b) when the verb is the subject of a clause

TRACK 05 / CD 1

c) when the verb is the object of a clause
d) after the verbs **like**, **love**, etc.
e) after **about**

1. I like **seeing** people, **meeting** people, **discussing** things with people.
2. The education is about **learning** how to use the brush.
3. **Seeing** a dental hygienist every six months... is enough?
4. How is that different from **being** a dentist?
5. The most important thing is **brushing** techniques.

VOCABULARY

6 Relacione os advérbios com a sua respectiva tradução.

> às vezes · normalmente · a cada seis meses · exatamente · eficientemente
> regularmente · de três a quatro vezes por dia · frequentemente · duas vezes ao ano
> corretamente · constantemente · devidamente · certamente · francamente

frankly	....	all the time	....
efficiently	....	properly	....
effectively	....	exactly	....
regularly	....	normally	....
often	....	every six months	....
three or four times a day	....	twice a year	....
correctly	....	sometimes	....

7 Coloque os advérbios anteriores na coluna correspondente.

Frequency (frequência)	Manner (modo)	Focusing (foco)

8 Complete o texto com os advérbios anteriores. Para cada caso há várias opções.

For Maria Elena, if you want to have healthy gums, seeing your dental hygienist (1) .... is important, but brushing your teeth (2) .... is also one of the most important things that you can do because a lot of people don't know how to brush their teeth (3) .... How (4) .... should you brush your teeth? Well, (5) .... is enough, but (6) .... , brushing your teeth (7) .... and (8) .... is much more important than how many times you do it. (9) .... patients who have periodontal disease have to see a dental hygienist more (10) ....

Take-away English

a little bit	um pouco
actually	de fato
and so on	etc.
different from*	diferente de / distinto de
instead of + Gerund	em vez de
What's wrong with...?	O que tem de mal em...?

* No inglês norte-americano, diz-se **different than**.

Glossary

actual	verdadeiro	hygienist	higienista
brush	escova	kind	tipo
brush (to)	escovar	made up of	que é feito de
cases	casos	patient	paciente
consist of (to)	consistir em	periodontal	periodontal
dental floss	fio dental	plaque	placa
depending	depende	prevent (to)	prevenir, evitar
discuss (to)	falar, discutir	right	correto, apropriado
do harm (to)	fazer mal	remove (to)	tirar
disease	enfermidade	role	papel, função
enough	suficiente	satisfied	satisfeito/a, contente
fillings	obturação	technique	técnica
for one thing	para começar	teeth	dentes
gum	gengiva	twice	duas vezes
healthy	saudável	underscore	sublinhar (sinal)
home-care	cuidados diários em casa	whole	inteiro, completo
		wrong	errado/a

Transcript

Brian: So Maria Elena, can you tell us a little bit about your work please?

Maria Elena: Well yes, I'd love to. My name is Maria Elena McCarthy. I'm a dental hygienist.

B: And how is that different from being a dentist?

M: Well we're educators. Our role is to educate and motivate the patient. The doctors or dentists do the actual work, fillings and so on.

B: Okay, you said education I mean – what do – what do people need to be educated to do?

M: Well frankly the most important thing is brushing techniques, home-care techniques, using the right brush, knowing how to brush efficiently and effectively, using dental floss, and coming to see me regularly.

B: Well what's wrong with the way most people brush their teeth?

M: They brush – and they brush often enough – I hear that all the time, three or four times a day, but their technique is wrong, and that creates problems in the mouth.

B: So what's wrong with the technique?

M: The technique is wrong because they don't use the brush correctly and they harm their teeth. Instead of helping, they actually do harm. The main thing that you have to do when you brush your teeth is to remove dental plaque correctly.

B: And what is dental plaque exactly?

M: Okay – dental plaque is made up of bacteria from the food you eat, and saliva.

B: So what does this education of patients consist of?

M: The education is about learning how to use the brush properly, home-care techniques, making it effective so that you have no disease, healthy gums and that way you prevent disease.

B: Right, and how often should people visit a dental hygienist?

M: Normally you should come every six months.

B: So, seeing a dental hygienist every six months, twice a year, is enough?

M: Well yes, but there are cases where people have to come every four months, sometimes even three months, depending. Often these are people who have a genetic problem – periodontal disease.

B: Periodontal disease?

M: Periodontal – yes, gum disease, these patients have to come more often.

B: Okay. What do you like about your work?

M: I like seeing people, meeting people, discussing things with people. I create a whole scenario, because I like people for one thing, and I'm here to help people, and that's really what it's all about.

B: Thank you very much, Maria Elena.

M: Thank you.

TRACK 06 / CD 1 ▶▶ RECIPE TIME

VOCABULARY

Food lexis

1 Relacione cada palavra com sua foto.

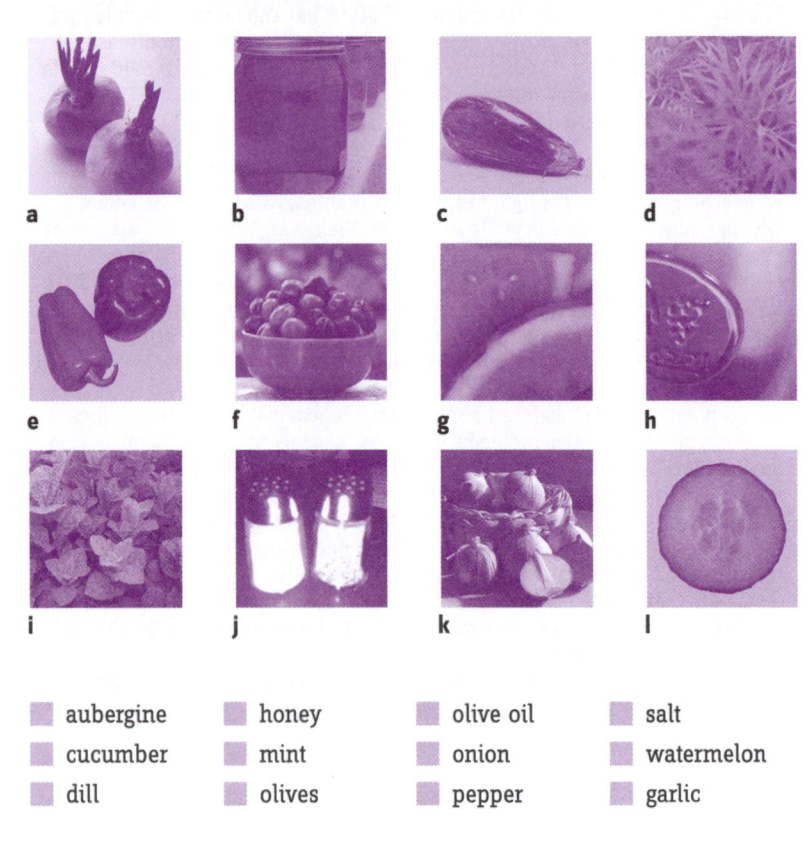

a   b   c   d

e   f   g   h

i   j   k   l

- aubergine
- cucumber
- dill
- honey
- mint
- olives
- olive oil
- onion
- pepper
- salt
- watermelon
- garlic

2 Coloque cada palavra em seu lugar correspondente. As palavras anteriores já estão colocadas. Use o dicionário ou consulte o glossário, se necessário.

> apple · bacon · banana · basil · beef · bread · butter · carrot · cheese · chicken cream · egg · flour · goat · grape · ham · kiwifruit · lemon · lamb · lettuce lobster · mandarin · margarine · melon · milk · mushroom · mussel · nuts octopus · oregano · parsley · pasta · peach · pork · potato · prawn · rosemary salmon · sardine · sole · squid · thyme · trout · turkey · veal · yoghurt · zucchini

fruit	vegetables	fish & seafood	meat	herbs & spices	dairy produce	other
watermelon	aubergine			dill		honey
	garlic			mint		olives
	onion			pepper		olive oil
	cucumber			salt		

CULTURAL note

In English-speaking countries the name of the same food can be different. This happens especially with fish, fruit and vegetables. For example, "abobrinha" in the UK is **courgette**, because the British learnt the word from the French, but in the USA, Australia and New Zealand it is known as **zucchini** because of contact with migrants from Italy. Similarly, in North America, "berinjela" is known as **eggplant** and in the UK it is known as **aubergine**, similar to French.

Cooking lexis

3 Relacione cada um destes verbos com sua tradução.

> boil · chop · drain · fry · grate · peel · mix · slice · serve

descascar	fritar	grelhar, ralar ....
misturar	servir	ferver ....
cortar (em cubos)	cortar em rodelas	escorrer ....

4 Faça o mesmo com os verbos abaixo.

> add · combine · cool · cook · dip · dry · leave · put · strain

secar	combinar	esfriar ....
cozinhar	acrescentar	coar ....
pôr, colocar	deixar	molhar, mergulhar ....

Em inglês, dizemos **make breakfast / lunch / dinner** quando nos referimos ao fato de preparar ou cozinhar. No entanto, dizemos **have** (ou **eat**) **breakfast / lunch / dinner** quando nos referimos a comer ou tomar algo.

I **make breakfast** for the children while they are getting ready for school.
It's quite normal for Americans to **have breakfast** in a bar on their way to work.
People like the French and the Spaniards still **have** a three-course **lunch**.

Dish, plate or course

A dish é um prato, uma comida: **My favourite dish is lasagne** ("Meu prato preferido é lasanha"). **Plate** é o objeto: **I've broken a plate!** ("Acabo de quebrar um prato!"). **Course** é um prato de comida dentro de um jantar ou almoço: **a three-course meal** ("um almoço de três pratos"). Diz-se **first course** ou **starter** ("primeiro prato"), **second course** ou **main course** ("segundo prato") e **dessert** ("sobremesa"). Mas **do the dishes** significa "lavar pratos". Uma pessoa que faz esse tipo de trabalho em um restaurante é um **dishwasher**. Este termo também é empregado para o lava-louças (o eletrodoméstico).

GRAMMAR

The imperative

Em inglês, o imperativo é formado com o infinitivo sem o **to**. Por exemplo: **Look!** ("Olhe!"). Só tem uma forma, utilizada tanto para o singular quanto para o plural, e para registros formais ou informais. Para construir a negação, basta acrescentar **Don't** ou **Do not** antes do verbo.

Drink this. It's good for you.
Connect the router to the back of the computer.
Don't be sarcastic with me!

É usado para dar instruções a alguém (ou geralmente para todo mundo):

Vote for the Green Party.
Switch off your computer when you finish working.
Do not speak during the exam.

Se quisermos ser um pouco menos diretos, podemos acrescentar **please** antes do verbo principal:

Please wait here until your number is called.
Passengers on Delta Airlines flight 345 to Los Angeles **please go** to gate 39.
Please don't tell Sara.

É usado também para explicar uma receita:

Peel and **chop** the garlic, **mix** it with the dried cucumber, **add** a bit of olive oil and a little bit of salt, and **combine** it all with the yoghurt.

Outra forma de explicar uma receita para alguém que temos diante de nós, é com **you**:

First **you chop** the watermelon into pieces, and **you dry** it a bit with kitchen paper.

LISTENING

5 Que ingredientes são mencionados nas receitas? Marque-os. Atenção! Há quatro deles que não são mencionados.

	Recipe 1 Katerina	Recipe 2 Daniela	Recipe 3 Eduardo
aubergine			
chicken			
cucumber			
dill			
eggs			
garlic			
honey			
melon			
mint			
olives			
olive oil			
onion			
parsley			
pepper			
potatoes			
ricotta cheese			
salt			
spaghetti			
tomatoes			
watermelon			
yoghurt			

6 Escute novamente a segunda receita e relacione os verbos com os nomes.

> slice · make · chop · add · fry · boil

.... the tomato sauce .... the tomatoes and onion
.... salt and pepper   .... the aubergines
.... the pasta   .... the aubergines

7 Escute a primeira receita, a do **tzatziki**, e complete o texto com os verbos.

First you **peel** the cucumber and .... it finely, and .... some salt on it and .... it for 15 minutes, so that the most of the water comes out. Then .... it with kitchen paper. Then .... and .... the garlic, ... it with the dried cucumber, ... a bit of olive oil and a little bit of salt, and .... it all with the yoghurt and the chopped dill. And you .... it in the fridge for a couple of hours.

CULTURAL note

In English-speaking countries food is not always given the same importance as it has in some parts of Brazil. The first meal of the day is called **breakfast** which is normally some kind of cereals (like cornflakes or muesli), milk or yoghurt, fruit juice, and tea or coffee. Breakfast is usually more substantial than in Brazil, and some people have a cooked breakfast (sometimes called British breakfast) which is a combination of hot food that can include fried eggs, bacon, sausages, fried tomatoes, baked beans, and fried mushrooms. At 12.00 or 1 pm people have **lunch**. This is usually a small meal, consisting of sandwiches, salad, soup, or a slice of pizza. People have their evening meal, usually called **dinner** (but some working class people in Britain and Ireland call it **tea**, and some middle class people call it **supper**) at home at any time from 5 pm to 8 pm, and this is the main meal of the day.

Glossary
breakfast: café da manhã **lunch:** almoço **tea:** jantar
dinner: jantar **supper:** jantar

Take-away English

All together.	Tudo junto.
And that's it!	E pronto!
Hang on.	Espere. *(informal)*
There's nothing like it!	Não há nada igual!
We'll be back.	Voltaremos.

Glossary

apple	maçã
bacon	bacon
banana	banana
basil	manjericão
beef	carne
bowl	tigela, bacia
bread	pão
butter	margarina
carrot	cenoura
check (to)	checar, verificar
cheese	queijo
chicken	frango
chips (o french fries)	batatas fritas
clove of garlic	um dente de alho
couple of (a)	duas
courgette	abobrinhas
cream	creme
cucumber	pepino
decorate (to)	decorar
dessert	sobremesa
dill	endro
dip	molho
dish	prato
egg	ovo
favourite	preferido/a
flour	farinha
fresh	fresco (não se emprega para temperatura)
fridge	geladeira
garlic	alho
get something out (to)	tirar
goat	cabrito
grape	uva
ham	presunto
honey	mel
ingredients	ingredientes
kitchen paper	papel de cozinha
kiwifruit	kiwi
knife	faca
lamb	cordeiro
leaves	folhas
lemon	limão
lettuce	alface
liquid	líquido
listener	ouvinte
lobster	lagosta
mandarin	tangerina
melon	melão
milk	leite
mint	hortelã, menta
mushroom	cogumelo, champignon
necessary	necessário/a
octopus	polvo
olive	azeitona
olive oil	azeite de oliva
onion	cebola
oregano	orégano
parsley	salsinha
pasta	macarrão
peach	pêssego
pepper	pimenta, pimentão
pieces	pedaços
pinch (a pinch of)	uma pitada (de)
plain	natural (iogurte)
pork	carne de porco
pot	panela
potato	batata
pronounce (to)	pronunciar
quarter	um quarto
recipe	receita (de cozinha)
ricotta	ricota
ripe	maduro/a *(comida)*
rosemary	alecrim
salmon	salmão
salt	sal
saucepan	caçarola
seeds	sementes
side	lado
sole	linguado
squid	lula
starter	primeiro prato
summer	verão
thyme	tomilho

tomato	tomate	veal	vitela
trout	truta	watermelon	melancia
turkey	peru	whole	integral
typical	típico/a, comum	yoghurt	iogurte
unsweetened	sem açúcar/adoçante	zucchini	abobrinha

Transcript

Sue: Recipe time! This is the spot where our listeners phone in with some of their favourite recipes. Our first caller is –
Katerina: Katerina from Southampton, but my family are from Greece.
S: So is this a Greek recipe.
K: Yes, it's a very typical starter, called Tztatziki.
S: Zaziki?
K: Tzatziki. It's easier to make than it is to pronounce, I tell you.
S: Well let's hope so.
K: Okay, the ingredients; unsweetened Greek yoghurt, and for two people let's say two pots. And then a cucumber, a clove of garlic, some olive oil, a pinch of salt and some fresh dill.
S: Sorry, Katerina – is the dill absolutely necessary?
K: Oh, yes it is. And it really needs to be fresh dill too. First you peel the cucumber and chop it finely, and put some salt on it and leave it for 15 minutes, so that most of the water comes out. Then dry it with kitchen paper. Then peel and chop the garlic, mix it with the dried cucumber, add a bit of olive oil and a little bit of salt, and combine it all with the yoghurt and the chopped dill. And you cool it in the fridge for a couple of hours.
S: And that's it?
K: Yes, if you want you can decorate it with a few black olives – Kalamata olives are the best – and a bit more dill. At home we make it all through the year, but it's especially good in summer as a starter.
S: And if you can't get dill?
K: Then use mint, but it has to be fresh mint.
S: Just one question, Katerina – how do you eat it?
K: Oh, it's a dip – you dip bread into it, or fried aubergines. Or chips if you're really ignorant.
S: Thanks you very much, Katerina. And our next caller is – ah – Daniela.
D: Hello?
S: Yes, Daniela, You're on air. Where are you from?
D: I'm from Catania, in Sicily.
S: Right, so are you going to give us a Sicilian recipe?
D: Yes, I'm going to give you my mother's recipe for *pasta alla norma*, It's a very typical Sicilian dish.
S: Right, so this is a main course. Now, what do you need to make it?
D: First of all 500 grams of spaghetti, then 1 kilo of ripe tomatoes, 200 grams of grated hard ricotta. And six large aubergines, three cloves of garlic, two onions, some fresh basil and olive oil.
S: Hang on, hang on, let's just check that: spaghetti 500 grams, ripe tomatoes 1 kilo, grated hard ricotta cheese

200 grams, six large aubergines, three cloves of garlic, two onions, fresh basil leaves, olive oil.

D: You slice the aubergines and put them in water with salt for one hour. Then you make the tomato sauce – chop the tomatoes and onion, and the whole garlic and the basil in a saucepan.

S: The whole garlic? You don't chop it?

D: That's right, the whole garlic. Then you add the fresh basil, and add salt and pepper. You cook that until the liquid has evaporated. Then you strain it, like a purée, and add olive oil. And you forget about that for a few minutes.

S: Now the aubergines, is that right?

D: Yes, you dry the aubergines in kitchen paper and fry them over a low heat, so that they're cooked on both sides. Then the pasta – boil the pasta in lots of salted water, and when it's cooked *al dente* you drain it with hot water. Now you serve it.

S: All together?

D: More or less. You serve the pasta with the ricotta then the sauce. Then mix it a little – you add the aubergines, more basil and then more ricotta. And that's it.

S: It sounds absolutely yummy. Delicious. Thanks a lot, Daniela.

D: You're welcome.

S: Right, that was Daniela from Italy. And now we have –

E: Hello, Sue.

S: Hi there, Eduardo. And where are you from, Eduardo?

E: I am from Madrid originally, but I live in Barcelona.

S: And what have you got for us today, Eduardo?

E: Well, it's a very simple summer dessert.

S: Sounds good. So what do you need?

E: First of all, you need a quarter of fresh watermelon, four pots of plain yoghurt – unsweetened Greek-style yoghurt is the best – some liquid honey, and some fresh mint leaves, chopped mint leaves I mean.

S: Let's just check that: watermelon – a big piece –, unsweetened Greek yoghurt – more Greek yoghurt! – four pots, liquid honey, and chopped fresh mint leaves. Mint, not dill?

E: What?

S: Mint, not dill?

E: Yes, that's right.

S: And how do you make it, Eduardo?

E: Well, first you chop the watermelon into pieces, not too small, and you dry it a bit with kitchen paper.

S: What about the seeds – you know those small brown seeds?

E: Well, if you can get them out with a knife, it's better. Okay, then when the watermelon is a bit dry, you mix everything together in a bowl–

S: The yoghurt, the liquid honey and the mint.

E: Yes, you can put a few mint leaves on top at the end, just for decoration. And then you leave it in the fridge for a couple of hours.

S: And that's it?

E: Yes, that's all there is to it.

S: It sounds incredibly easy. Thanks very much, Eduardo.

E: You're welcome.

S: That was Eduardo from Madrid, and Barcelona. And our producer tells me that that's all we have time for today. Our thanks go to all our callers, especially if you didn't have time to go on air today, but we'll be back same time next week.

TRACK 07 / CD 1 ▶▶ ROB IN THE UK

LISTENING

1 Em geral, a estadia de Rob na Grã-Bretanha foi **a good or a bad experience**? Por quê? Coloque um G (de **good**), um B (de **bad**) ou um X, caso ele não mencione nada, ao lado de cada tema.

- ▢ his flat
- ▢ his work
- ▢ the people at work
- ▢ the cities
- ▢ the summers
- ▢ his salary
- ▢ the food
- ▢ parties
- ▢ the parks
- ▢ the winters
- ▢ public transport
- ▢ football

2 Rob trabalha em quê? Marque a opção correta.

Rob is...
- ▢ a) a biologist
- ▢ b) a pharmacist
- ▢ c) a farmer
- ▢ d) an economist

3 True or false? Corrija as que sejam falsas.

	true	false
1. He had lunch in a pub.		
2. He used public transport.		
3. He worked eight hours a day.		
4. He worked for a big company.		
5. He didn't work in the same place every day.		
6. He met his friends for lunch.		
7. He went to bed at 10.30.		

4 Marque os lugares que são mencionados por Rob.

- ▢ Newcastle
- ▢ Dublin
- ▢ York
- ▢ Edinburgh
- ▢ London
- ▢ Glasgow
- ▢ Durham
- ▢ Liverpool

5 Preste atenção nas frases abaixo e marque as palavras ou as sílabas que são pronunciadas com maior ênfase. Em seguida, pronuncie cada uma imitando a entonação, a pronúncia e onde houver junção de sílabas.

1. No, I didn't. I lived in Newcastle, in the northeast of England.
2. I lived there for nearly two years. Then I returned to the States.
3. What I liked was the job that I had.
4. What I didn't like was the freezing, dark winters, and their food.
5. In my free time I did lots of things.
6. I loved staying at home and reading a book, or sometimes I cooked nice Mexican food for my friends.

VOCABULARY

6 Marque os verbos que já apareceram em unidades anteriores.

- became
- chose
- cooked
- did
- finished
- gave
- had
- learned
- liked
- lived
- made
- met
- needed
- phoned
- realised
- thought
- travelled
- wanted
- watched
- was/were
- went
- woke up

7 Escreva ao lado de cada infinitivo seu equivalente no **simple past** em inglês.

> became · chose · did · finished · emigrated · gave · learned · liked · lived · made met · needed · called/phoned · realised · travelled · watched · woke up

1. aprender ....
2. escolher ....
3. fazer ....
4. fazer ....
5. viver ....
6. encontrar-se com ....
7. dar ....
8. emigrar ....
9. acordar ....
10. terminar ....
11. converter-se em ....
12. ligar, telefonar ....
13. dar-se conta ....
14. gostar ....
15. necessitar ....
16. viajar ....
17. ver, olhar ....

8 Como é construído o **simple past** dos verbos regulares? Coloque os verbos anteriores na coluna correspondente.

Regular pasts	Irregular pasts

Do or make?

9 Como você percebeu, "fazer" em inglês pode ser tanto **do** quanto **make**. Sublinhe (**underline**) a opção correta em cada caso.

1. Then he **did** / **made** a very strange thing.
2. I **did** / **made** French, not English, at school.
3. Please don't **do** / **make** a noise – the children are asleep.
4. Could you **do** / **make** a copy of this for me?
5. I don't have time to **do** / **make** my homework, I'm afraid.
6. Let's **do** / **make** a plan.
7. I like **doing** / **making** nothing.
8. What do you want to **do** / **make** tomorrow?
9. She's **doing** / **making** a Master's in Psychology.
10. I'm not going to **do** / **make** any work today.
11. On Sunday I often **do** / **make** a cake.

Agora, complete as regras. Marque o verbo que é usado em cada caso. O mais importante é aprender quais palavras são (**collocate**) com **make** e quais são com **do**.

- We normally use **do** / **make** for producing, causing, creating, constructing, performing...
- We use **do** / **make** for indefinite activities.
- We normally use **do** / **make** for an action. We also use it when we don't say exactly what activity we're talking about – for example with words like *thing, something, nothing, anything, what*.
- We use **do** / **make** when we talk about work, jobs or subjects of study.

See or watch?

Rob diz: **I went home and I watched TV**. Na faixa anterior, Karen disse: **That was really interesting because we saw whales, seals and even dolphins**. Usamos **see** para nos referir a algo que vemos com nossos próprios olhos, em geral porque simplesmente está na nossa frente.

Can you **see** the car coming up behind you?
You can **see** the volcano from most places on the island.

Também usamos **see** para um filme, uma peça de teatro, um jogo etc.

Did you **see** the match last night?
No, I was at the cinema. I **saw** a really old but really good Woody Allen film.

Usamos **watch** para algo que está acontecendo neste exato momento ou que está a ponto de ocorrer.

Watch that woman; she's acting suspiciously.

Também usamos **watch** para falar da televisão em geral, e indistintamente **see** ou **watch** para programas ou filmes específicos.

Watching TV is what most people do in the evening.
Could you phone me later? I'm **watching** Chelsea against Arsenal on the TV.
I **watched / saw** the news last night – what's happening in Asia is incredible!
Did you **see** *Big Brother* on Saturday? No, I don't **watch** much TV.

Subway or metro / Apartment or flat / Football or soccer

Em inglês americano, diz-se **subway** e em inglês britânico, **metro** (embora em Londres se diga **the tube**). Em inglês britânico, **a subway** é uma passagem subterrânea. Em inglês americano, diz-se **apartment**, no britânico, **flat**. E o **football** nos Estados Unidos é conhecido como **soccer**.

Store or shop?

Nos Estados Unidos é comum usar **store** e na Grã-Bretanha, **shop**. No entanto, frequentemente, os canais de televisão (como o de Rob) usam a palavra **store**. **Store** e **shop** também são verbos: **to store** significa "armazenar" e **to shop**, "comprar (em uma loja)".

Town or city?

A diferença entre **towns** e **cities** varia de acordo com o país. De fato, muitas línguas têm uma única palavra: *ville* em francês, *Stadt* em alemão, *città* en italiano, *ciudad* en espanhol etc.). Já nos países de fala anglo-saxã não existe uma definição única para **city**. Na Grã-Bretanha **a city** deve ter pelo menos uma catedral, na Nova Zelândia deve ter pelo menos 50 mil habitantes e nos Estados Unidos a definição varia de acordo com o estado. Em geral, se uma área urbana tem mais de 200 mil habitantes, pode ser considerada **a city**.

10 Complete as frases com estes verbos. Nem todos serão necessários.

> became · chose · cooked · finished · gave · had · learned · liked · lived · made
> met · needed · phoned · realised · thought · travelled · went · woke up

1. Filippo _____ a beautiful *spaghetti alla carbonara* for dinner.
2. Luciana _____ in Buenos Aires until the age of 28.
3. I _____ you three times on Saturday. Where were you?
4. She _____ to the gym four times a week last year. Now, she goes less.
5. I _____ my husband when I was doing a language course.
6. He _____ a decision never to return to Cuba.
7. I _____ at 04.00, when the telephone rang.
8. When she _____ that Economics was not for her, she changed to Law.
9. "Who _____ you this painting?" "It was a present from my first wife."
10. Spain and Portugal _____ part of the European Community in 1984.

CULTURAL note

Compared to young people in Continental Europe, many young people in Britain drink an enormous amount of alcohol on Friday and Saturday nights. A lot of people drink to **get drunk**. Young women in the 18-26 **age** group in the UK now consume more units of alcohol per week than young men of the same age. Town centres can be **dangerous** places, with **increasing drunkenness**, anti-social **behaviour** and alcohol-related violence now becoming common. This is recognised as a **major** social problem in Britain. The ambulance service and police are very **busy** on Fridays and Saturdays, and **attempts** by the Government to control the problem are not **usually successful**.

Glossary

age: idade	perigoso	**major**: grande
attempts: tentativas	**drunkenness**: embriaguez, alcoolismo	**successful**: bem-sucedido
behaviour: comportamento	**enormous**: enorme	**to get drunk**: embebedar-se
busy: ocupado	**increasing**: crescente	**units**: unidades
dangerous:		**usually**: normalmente

Take-away English

What was it like?	Como foi? / Como era?
to give a hand	dar uma ajuda / dar uma mão
Thanks for doing that.	Obrigada por fazer isso.
My pleasure.	Foi um prazer.
I never got used to it.	Nunca me acostumei (com isso).

Glossary

a lot of	muito/a, muitos/as	country	país
after	depois (de)	daily	de cada dia
amount	quantidade *(não contável)*	dark	escuro/a
ancestors	antepassados	decide (to)	decidir
another	outro/a	different	diferente
apartment (US)	apartamento	drink (to)	beber
around	ao redor de	especially	principalmente
become true (to)	tornar realidade	even	inclusive
bed	cama	every	cada
beer	cerveja	far away from	muito longe de
call (to)	ligar, telefonar	finish (to)	terminar
chance	oportunidade	flat (UK)	apartamento
child	criança, filho/a	follow (to)	seguir
choose (to)	escolher	food	comida
city	cidade	football	futebol
coffee	café	freezing	muito frio/a, gelado/a
company	empresa	friend	amigo/a
cook (to)	cozinhar	girlfriend	namorada

give (to)	dar	pharmacist	farmacêutico/a
go jogging (to)	sair para correr	program (US)	programa (*em inglês britânico é* **programme**)
go out (to)	sair (para jantar, dançar etc.)		
go to the movies (to)	ir ao cinema	quite	bastante
		read (to)	ler
gym	academia	really	realmente
hand	mão	reason	razão
home	lar, casa	scary	de medo
meet (to)	encontrar-se, marcar com	soccer (US)	futebol
large	grande	sometimes	às vezes
live (to)	viver	stay at home (to)	ficar em casa
lots of	muitos/as	store (US)	loja
love (to)	amar, querer	subway (US)	metrô
lovely	bonito/a, adorável	theatre (UK)	teatro (*em inglês norte-americano se escreve* **theater**)
mind	mente		
nearly	quase		
need (to)	precisar	thesis	monografia (de mestrado)
nice	bom/boa, simpático/a	travel (to)	viajar
of course	claro que sim	wake up (to)	acordar
open (to)	abrir	watch TV (to)	ver televisão
opportunities	oportunidades	weekly	semanal
park	parque	winter	inverno

Transcript

Sue: Well thanks for that. Now we've got Brian talking to somebody who lived in the UK. Brian, are you there?
Brian: Yeah. Hello Sue.
S: Okay, Brian, you're on.
B: Thanks Sue. With me I've got Rob. Rob, thanks for agreeing to talk to us.
Rob: My pleasure.
B: So why did you decide to go and live in Britain?
R: Well, even when I was a child I really wanted to live and work in another country and one day this dream became true. The reason why I chose the UK was because – well – I realised that I had real work opportunities there and, as well, I thought that it was a great chance to see where my family originally came from. They emigrated to the US about 150 years ago.
B: A lot of people go to London to live, but you didn't, did you?
R: No, I didn't. I lived in Newcastle, in the northeast of England. I lived in a great apartment – well, they don't say *apartment*, they say *flat* – not far away from the city centre.
B: And what was it like?
R: It was a great experience that really made me open my mind a lot. I think I learned a lot about British culture, and I had the chance to meet English people of course, but also other people from all over the world. And of course to go see where my ancestors lived.
B: How long did you live there?

R: I lived there for nearly two years. Then I returned to the States.
B: Two years is a good amount of time to see what you liked and what you didn't like.
R: What I liked was the job that I had, working as a pharmacist, and the lovely people who I met, especially the people from work who gave me a hand anytime I needed it, and for everything that I needed and, of course, another thing that I liked was the cities – with good public transport – and the really beautiful parks they have.
B: Right and what didn't you like so much?
R: Well, what I didn't like was the freezing, dark winters, and the food, I never got used to it. And the people drink so much – every Friday and Saturday night people go out and drink an incredible amount of beer. It was quite scary sometimes.
B: I can imagine. What was your daily or weekly routine?
R: Well, let's see. Normally, I woke up at around 7:30 and I made my breakfast and my lunch – because I had that at work. I travelled by subway – they call it the *metro* – and I was at work from 9 o'clock until 6:00 pm. I worked for a large pharmaceutical company that has a lot of stores in the UK and I had a weekly program that I had to follow, and I went to a different store every day – the company has lots of stores around Newcastle. When I finished work, and depending on the day, I went jogging, or I worked on my thesis, met my friends, or I went home and I watched TV, then I had dinner, I called my family and my girlfriend back home, and I went to bed around 11:30.
B: What did you do in your free time?
R: In my free time I did lots of things, for example, after work I met my friends for coffee or a drink. On Fridays or Saturdays I went to the movies and sometimes to the theatre, and to see Newcastle United play.
B: Aha!
R: Yes, Brian, I even learned to liked soccer – oh, sorry, *football*! On the weekend and days off, I travelled to other cities, like Edinburgh, Durham, York, or even Dublin, but I loved staying at home and reading a book, or sometimes I cooked nice Mexican food for my friends.
B: Thanks a lot, Rob.
R: Any time, Brian.

TRACK 08 / CD 1 ▶▶ **THE OLYMPIC GAMES**

LISTENING

1 Quem fez o quê? Una as diferentes partes para formar quatro frases.

At the	1984 1976 2008 1972	Olympic Games winter Olympics	Nadia Comaneci Torvill and Dean Mark Spitz Michael Phelps	won eight gold medals. scored a perfect score of 10. won seven gold medals. had 12 maximum points from all 12 judges.

2 Marque a pessoa que fala de cada um destes Jogos Olímpicos. Em um caso, há duas pessoas que comentam.

	Juliet	Stuart	Sue
1. The 1972 Munich Olympics			
2. The 1976 Montreal Olympics			
3. The 1984 Sarajevo winter Olympics			
4. The 1992 Barcelona Olympics			
5. The 2008 Beijing Olympics			

3 Agora, tente responder a estas perguntas em seu caderno... em inglês!

1. How many times did Nadia Comaneci score maximum points?
2. What was unusual about the winter Olympics in Yugoslavia?
3. Why didn't Jane Torvill and Christopher Dean dance in the 1988 Games?
4. Why made Sue cry at the 1992 Games?

4 Aproximadamente 50% das palavras inglesas provêm do latim ou do grego. Nesta faixa aparecem muitas palavras que se parecem muito com seus equivalentes em português, mas são pronunciadas de forma um pouco diferente. Escute o programa e marque as que são pronunciadas com maior ênfase. Em seguida, pratique sua pronúncia repetindo estas frases.

1. For me one of the interesting things about the Olympics...
2. ... that's a bit more philosophical than I was expecting...
3. The Montreal Olympics were famous for a young girl from Romania...
4. She was 14 years old at the time, she won several titles in the field of gymnastics and she scored a perfect score of 10.
5. ... they became professional after the 1984 games, and then they couldn't compete in the Olympics...
6. I've seen some incredible athletes...
7. ... but the most moving, the most emotional moment for me was the opening ceremony of the 1992 Olympics in Barcelona.

VOCABULARY

5 Escreva ao lado da palavra em português seu equivalente em inglês. Observe que há muitas palavras que se parecem e algumas que são iguais.

> archery · athletics · badminton · basketball · billiards · boxing · canoeing
> cycling · diving · fencing · football · golf · gymnastics · hockey · jogging · judo
> motorcycle racing · rowing · rugby · sailing · ski-ing · squash · swimming
> table-tennis · tennis · triathlon · weightlifting · wrestling

atletismo		ciclismo	
hóquei		motociclismo	
tênis de mesa		vela	
boxe		*badminton*	
esgrima		tênis	
squash		futebol	
tiro ao alvo		ginástica	
judô		luta	
canoagem		remo	
triatlo		esqui	
bilhar		basquete	

rúgbi	....	natação	....
golfe	....	caminhada	....
levantamento de peso	....	saltos ornamentais	....

6 Que esportes mencionados anteriormente são usados com o verbo **play**? São 10.

play + ▭ ▭ ▭ ▭ ▭ ▭ ▭ ▭ ▭ ▭

O que eles têm em comum? Complete a frase.

They all have a .... and they are all competition sports (an individual versus an individual or a team versus a team) and they all have goals or points.

7 Quais dos esportes mencionados anteriormente são usados com o verbo **go**? São 7.

go + ▭ ▭ ▭ ▭ ▭ ▭ ▭

O que eles têm em comum? Complete a frase.

They all end in -.......... and they are all about movement (going from A to B).

Sport or exercise?

O que fazemos em uma **gym** ("academia") ou em um **fitness centre** para ficar em forma (**to keep fit**) é chamado de **exercise** ("exercício"). **Exercise** inclui também **jogging** ou **cycling**. Se você não está muito em forma, seu médico provavelmente vai dizer para você fazer exercício (**do** ou **get some exercise**). A palavra **sport** implica algum tipo de competição: **You see sport on TV all the time but it is very unusual to see exercise on TV**.

The Olympics

Nos Jogos Olímpicos (**Olympic Games**), o terceiro lugar ganha medalha de bronze, o que fica em segundo ganha medalha de prata e o vencedor, medalha de ouro. No final da cerimônia de entrega das medalhas, toca o hino nacional (**the national anthem**). Em alguns casos, os melhores atletas quebram o recorde mundial (**break the world record**) ou estabelecem um novo recorde do mundo (**set a new world record**).

GRAMMAR

The present perfect

8 Sue pergunta para Stuart: **Have you ever been to the Olympics?** E ele responde: **I've been to the Olympics twice**. Marque a opção correta.

They are talking about...
a) some time in the past
b) the present
c) the future

9 Agora, complete a regra com duas destas opções: **is/are**, **have/has**, **do/does**, **present participle**, **past participle**.

> The present perfect consists of two elements: the auxiliary verb .... and the ....

Usamos o **present perfect** em alguns casos específicos:

a) Para nos referirmos a fatos recentes muito vinculados ao presente.

The government **has offered** help to young people trying to buy a house.
Sarah **has** just **cut** her hair – it looks great.

b) Para nos referirmos a fatos que ocorreram no passado, mas sem defini-lo.

They**'ve been** to India three times.*
"**Have** you **seen** Pulp Fiction?" "Yes, I have."**

c) Para nos referirmos a fatos que começaram em um momento determinado do passado e que continuam no presente.

France **has** always **been** a very centralist state.
My parents **have lived** in this house since they got married.

* Coloquialmente, é comum o uso da forma contraída do auxiliar.
** Costuma-se dar respostas curtas sem o **past participle**: **Yes, I have / No, we haven't**.

10 Relacione cada frase com um dos usos mencionados anteriormente.

1. "How long have you been divorced?" "For three years."
2. I've never eaten guacamole, because I don't like avocado.
3. Liverpool FC have been one of England's top clubs for many years.
4. Blanca has just told me some very important news.
5. Have you ever watched a complete opera?
6. Mum! I've passed the Physics exam! I can't believe it!
7. Brazil has been a democracy since the mid 1980s.
8. Police say there has been an explosion outside the Town Hall.
9. Sarah, I have to confess that I've always loved you.
10. Have you ever drunk *rabo de galo*?

Em que caso é usada cada uma das palavras abaixo? Indique a letra.

▪ since   ▪ How long   ▪ ever
▪ just   ▪ for

The passive voice

Stuart diz: **And she was crowned Olympic Champion for the 1976 games**. Sabemos quem a coroou? É relevante o nome da pessoa que a coroou? A resposta a essas duas perguntas é "não".

11 Agora, complete a regra com duas destas palavras: **to be**, **to have**, **to do**, **present participle**, **past participle**.

> The passive voice consists of two elements: the auxiliary verb
> .... and the ....

A voz passiva é muito comum tanto no inglês quanto no português! Em ambas as línguas, usa-se a voz passiva para o passado, para o presente ou para o futuro.

Present simple passive:	They **are held** every four years.
Simple past passive:	Where **were** those games **held**?
Present perfect passive:	That was the only time that the winter Olympics **have been held** in a communist country.
Future simple passive:	Do you know where the next winter Olympics **will be held**?

12 Complete estas frases com o verbo na voz passiva.

1. These cars _____ (**make**) in Mexico. *(present simple)*

2. All flights from Congonhas _____ (**delay**) because of the poor visibility in São Paulo. *(past simple)*

4. This question _____ (**consider**) by the government. *(present perfect)*

3. Is it true that the next Woody Allen film _____ (**make**) in Australia? *(future)*

Take-away English

... and what have you	... e outros
As I was saying...	Como ia dizendo...
I didn't mean that actually.	Na verdade, não queria dizer isso.
It brought tears to my eyes.	Me fez chorar.
It was out of this world.	Foi incrível.
the only time	a única vez
What do you think of them/it?	O que você acha deles/disso?

CULTURAL note

Stuart says: "… and of course the Commonwealth Games have been in Canada." After the Olympics, The Commonwealth Games is the world's biggest, multinational, multi-sport event. **It is held** every four years. The first event, then known as the British Empire Games, was held in 1930 in Hamilton, Ontario, Canada. The modern name of the Commonwealth Games was first used in 1974. As well as many Olympic sports, the Games also include some sports that are played **mainly** in Commonwealth countries. There are **currently** 53 members of the Commonwealth, and 71 teams participate in the Games.

Glossary

currently: atualmente	it is held: se celebra	mainly: principalmente

Glossary

actually	na verdade	field	campo, área
age	idade	fireworks	fogos de artifício
amateur	amador	forever	para sempre
amazing	incrível	games	jogos
archer	arqueiro	gold	ouro
arrow	flecha	greatest	o melhor
artistry	maestria, arte	hostage	refém
athlete	atleta	ice skating	patinação no gelo
beauty	beleza	incredible	incrível
become (to)	tornar-se	judge	juiz
brilliant	genial, brilhante	light	luz
captivate (to)	cativar	life	vida
ceremony	cerimônia	live	ao vivo
champion	campeão/ã	massacre	massacre
compete (to)	competir	medal	medalha
country	país	memories	recordações
creative	criativo/a	moving	comovente
crisis	crise	no longer	não mais
crown (to)	coroar	opening	inauguração, abertura
cry (to)	chorar	perform (to)	atuar
dance (to)	dançar	philosophical	filosófico/a
dancer	bailarino/a	remember (to)	lembrar-se de
entire	inteiro/a	rules	regras
every	cada	score	resultado, placar, pontuação
expect (to)	esperar		
experience (to)	viver, experimentar	several	vários/as
explode (to)	explodir	shoot (to)	atirar, lançar, chutar
famous	famoso/a, celebridade	skill	habilidade, destreza

spectacular	espetacular	tour	volta
stay (to)	permanecer, ficar	twice	duas vezes
success	sucesso	winter	inverno
such	tão	win (to)	ganhar (*no esporte, concurso, jogo*)
swimmer	nadador/a	world	mundial, mundo
tear	lágrima	wrong	errado/a
theatrical	teatral	young	jovem
through	através de		

Transcript

Sue: The Olympic games. What do you think of them? For me, you know, I think it's the only time I really like watching TV.

Stuart: For me one of the interesting things about the Olympics is – you know, because they're held every four years, and held in a different city every time, even held in a different country, you have such distinct memories about them. What I mean is – you remember them differently because you're a different age, you've become four years older, and probably your life has changed since the last Olympics.

S: Wow, that's a bit more philosophical than I was expecting, Stuart!

St: Well, you know, it's something I've always thought when it comes to the Olympics.

S: And what's the greatest memory of the Olympic Games for you?

St: Do you mean have I ever been to the Olympics?

S: No, I didn't mean that actually, but anyway, have you ever been to the Olympics?

St: I've been to the Olympics twice in fact – in Montreal in 1976, when I was quite young, and in Barcelona in 1992.

S: And what's the thing that you remember most about the Montreal Olympics?

St: First that it was great for Canada. It's the only time the Olympics have been in Canada – well, the main Olympics, I mean, the winter Olympics have been in Canada, and of course the Commonwealth Games have been in Canada.

S: The Montreal Olympics were famous for a young girl from Romania called –

St: Nadia Comaneci, yeah, exactly. And she was 14 years old at that time, she won several titles in the field of gymnastics and she scored a perfect score of 10, she was the first gymnast ever to do that I think, and if I'm not wrong she did it six times at the Montreal games. Since then the rules have changed, so her record will stay intact in theory forever.

S: Yeah – I remember her. She moved so beautifully, and she completely captivated the entire world with her ability and her success.

St: And she was crowned Olympic Champion for the 1976 games.

S: That's right. Well, thanks, Stuart. What about you, Jules?

Juliet: Well the Olympic champions that have always stayed in my mind were two British ice skating cham-

pions, Jane Torvill and Christopher Dean.
S: Ah, they were brilliant! That was in the – what was it? – the 1984 winter Olympics.
J: Yeah, that's right, the 1984 winter Olympics.
St: Where were those games held?
J: They were held in Sarajevo, in Bosnia, and that was the only time that the winter Olympics have been held in a communist country.
St: Because Bosnia was part of Yugoslavia at that time.
J: That's right. And Jane Torvill and Christopher Dean became the highest scoring ice skaters of all time. They got twelve perfect sixes. Twelve, from twelve different judges. That was incredible.
S: It's amazing.
J: And that had never happened before and it has never happened since then.
S: That's right; a six is the highest score that you can get, isn't it?
St: And I don't think they danced in the 1988 games, but I can't remember why.
J: The thing is, they became professional after the 1984 games, and then they couldn't compete in the Olympics any more –
S: Because they were no longer amateurs, right. And did you see them perform, Jules?
J: They did a world tour and I saw that in London. I saw them skate live and I was amazed by their skill, their artistry and beauty on ice, really, it brought tears to my eyes. I've never seen anything so beautiful, anywhere.
St: And what's your greatest moment in Olympic sport, Sue?
S: Well I've seen some incredible athletes, like the incredible Mark Spitz in Munich in 1972, who won I think seven gold –
J: Oh Munich in 1972 was the worst moment I've ever experienced in the Olympics –
St: Ok, was that because of the hostage crisis?
S: Oh, god, yes, that horrible massacre of Israeli athletes. Who could forget that? But anyway, as I was saying – the incredible Mark Spitz in Munich, who won I think seven gold medals, and there was another American swimmer Michael Phelps *(she actually says Mark Phelps)*, who won eight in Beijing in 2008, but the most moving, the most emotional moment for me was the opening ceremony of the 1992 Olympics in Barcelona.
St: Why? Why was that?
S: Because I was living in Barcelona at the time, and I saw the event live in the stadium, and I've never seen something so spectacular and – er – artistic, as that ceremony.
J: Do you remember when the archer shot an arrow through – what was it?
S: Yeah, through an arc that had gas or something in it, and it exploded into light. It was so emotional, it was out of this world. I cried. I'm telling you, I cried.
J: Yeah, it was the Olympic flame.
St: That was really something, wasn't it?
S: And the beauty, the creative, theatrical beauty of the ceremony has always stayed with me, I'll never forget it. And I've seen more spectacular opening ceremonies, with more lights, and more lasers, and fireworks, and dancers and what have you, but I've never seen a more artistic one.
J: Ah, isn't that nice?

TRACK 09 / CD 1 ▶▶ HOROSCOPES

LISTENING

1 Ouça os primeiros 20 segundos do texto e complete o quadro.

Who believes in horoscopes?	yes	no
Sue		
Stuart		
Brian		
Juliet		

2 Agora, ouça o resto do texto e complete o quadro da página seguinte com as características positivas e negativas que faltam de cada signo (uma em cada coluna). Sugerimos que dê uma pausa depois de cada signo.

Positive characteristics		Negative characteristics	
Column 1	Column 2	Column 3	Column 4
charming	adventurous	cool	can't focus on the real world
enthusiastic	dynamic	dislikes fantasy	doesn't always finish things
generous	enjoys helping others	impulsive	focuses on very small things
good in teams	imaginative	involved in lots of things	overemotional
idealistic	intense	jealous	possessive
independent	lives for the people he/she loves	protective	secretive
open	optimistic	secretive	
trusting	responsible	pompous	
values the family	warm	too analytical	

Star sign	Positive characteristics		Negative characteristics	
	Column 1	Column 2	Column 3	Column 4
Aquarius				**unemotional**
Pisces		**sensitive**		
Aries				
Taurus			**stubborn**	
Gemini	**energetic**			
Cancer		**private**		
Leo				**bossy**
Virgo			**too perfectionist**	
Libra		**likes balance**		
Scorpio	**adaptable**			
Sagittarius			**too direct**	
Capricorn	**patient**			

VOCABULARY

Dependent prepositions

Os verbos abaixo sempre regem a mesma preposição.

to believe in something or someone
to focus on something or someone
to tend to (do) something
to spend time (or money) on something or someone

3 Sem olhar os verbos acima, preencha com a preposição adequada.

1. People here tended _____ give their children presents on January 6th, but this is changing now.
2. I'd like today to focus _____ the question of domestic violence.
3. Do you believe _____ God?
4. We spent R$ 2000 _____ this PC four years ago and now we have to change it.

Adjectives for personality

4 Os adjetivos abaixo foram retirados do texto. Sublinhe (**underline**) a sílaba tônica.

adaptable	adventurous	ambitious	balanced	big-hearted
bossy	calm	careful	charming	confident
direct	dogmatic	dynamic	energetic	enthusiastic
honest	idealistic	impulsive	instinctive	intense
inventive	jealous	motivated	open	optimistic
passionate	patient	playful	pompous	possessive
private	protective	responsible	secretive	stable
stubborn	trusting	warm		

Você pode procurar o significado no glossário no final do texto, mesmo que a maioria apresente formas similares em português. Em seguida, tente responder a estas perguntas:

Which five do you think are most true about you?
Think of a friend. Which five do you think are most true about him/her?
Which are the five most important for being the leader of a country?
Which are the five most important for a close friend?
Which are the five most important for being a manager?

5 Preencha cada caso com um dos adjetivos.

Somebody...
1. who doesn't reject new ideas is:
2. who likes giving orders is:
3. who does a lot of things is: or
4. with very strong feelings is   or
5. whose opinions are very fixed is:
6. who considers different options carefully is:
7. who acts before thinking much is: or
8. who thinks that good things will happen is:
9. who talks to people about private questions is:
10. who doesn't want you to have other friends is: or

Adverbs of manner

A maioria dos advérbios de modo se forma com o acréscimo da terminação **-ly** ao adjetivo. Normalmente vem depois do verbo.

Life will **get better financially**.
The simple solution is to **make decisions** more **quickly**.
... because you won't be **thinking clearly** enough.

GRAMMAR

Future

Empregamos as formas **will** e **won't** (**will not**) para nos referir a coisas que ocorrerão (ou que não ocorrerão, no caso de **won't**) no futuro. Se não temos certeza, podemos acrescentar **I think** ("eu acho"), **maybe** ou **perhaps** ("talvez"). A estrutura é sempre a mesma:

> **will** / **won't** + infinitive (without **to**)

Quando o sujeito é um pronome pessoal, normalmente é empregada a forma contraída: **I'll**, **we'll** etc.

Belinda **will be** here at 10 o'clock.
Next year I think **we'll have** more problems.

O futuro também é muito utilizado para levantar hipóteses:

Will I be happy, will I be rich?
Will the government survive this new crisis?

Também empregamos **will** tanto para oferecimentos espontâneos quanto para expressar uma decisão ou uma solução para uma circunstância ou problemas novos.

Give me the keys, darling. **I'll** drive.
If what you say is true, **we'll** have to change our plans.
There's no white wine? Oh well, **I'll** have a beer instead.

Pode ainda ser empregado para pedir a alguém, de forma coloquial, que faça algo.

Will you answer the phone please?
Will you turn the music down? I'm trying to study.

6 Escute novamente o texto e relacione os signos com as previsões.

> Aquarius · Pisces · Aries · Taurus · Gemini · Cancer · Leo
> Virgo · Libra · Scorpio · Sagittarius · Capricorn

1. Will need to do things very simply because of problems with technology.
2. Will need to hear a lot of opinions that are different from your own.
3. Will have problems trying to make everyone happy.
4. Will need to spend a lot of time with other people.
5. Will have problems if you try to do too many things.
6. Will possibly offend someone by being too dogmatic.
7. Will feel that other people don't understand you.
8. Will have to balance being alone with being social.
9. Will need to focus on health questions.
10. Will have a good week for romance.
11. Will tend to analyse different options too much.
12. Will need to be careful not to get involved in other people's money problems.

7 Ouça estes fragmentos e veja como são pronunciados **will** e **won't**.

This week, **you'll try** to make everyone happy, but it **won't be** easy, so spend your time only on the people who **will appreciate** you.
This week, technology **will cause** you some real problems.
In the next few days **you'll feel** your best, so **you'll benefit** by spending more time socialising. Go to a party, meet people, you **won't regret** it.

Take-away English

* Let's start with...	Vamos começar com...
Stay calm.	Fique calmo.
to see the big picture	ter uma visão geral das coisas
to lead others by one's example	ser um exemplo para os demais

* Let's +infinitivo é uma forma de fazer sugestões e propostas.

CULTURAL note

In his first **press conference** after his election, President Barack Obama mentioned that he had talked to all of the **living former** Presidents, as "I didn't want to **get into** a Nancy Reagan thing about, you know, doing any séances." he had to **apologise** for the reference to the former **First Lady** Nancy Reagan. San Francisco-based astrologer Joan Quigley had become Nancy's personal astrologer in the 1970s, and she later had special private phone lines installed in the White House and at Camp David, **expressly** for talking to Quigley. **Shortly after** the assassination **attempt** on President Reagan, Quigley said that she could have **warned** Nancy that the President's **charts foretold** a bad day, but Nancy hadn't phoned her that day. Donald Regan, then President Reagan's **Chief of Staff** complained that virtually every **major move** and decision the Reagans made was **checked in advance** with their astrologer, who **drew up** horoscopes to **make certain** that the planets were in a favorable **alignment** for whatever the President was planning to do. But former Democrat First Lady Hillary Clinton also had séances in the White House. *Washington* Post reporter Bob Woodward described how Hillary Clinton consulted with a spiritual **adviser** who **guided** her through "conversations" with her personal heroine, Eleanor Roosevelt. *Newsweek* magazine, which was promoting Woodward's book, described the visits as "séances", an expression that the White House **quickly** tried to **suppress**.

Glossary

adviser:	conselheiro/a
alignment:	alinhamento
attempt:	tentativa
apologise (to):	pedir desculpas
chart:	mapa astral
check (to):	checar, verificar
Chief of Staff:	chefe de gabinete
complain (to):	queixar-se
draw up (to):	redigir, escrever
expressly:	expressamente
former:	antigo, ex
First Lady:	primeira-dama
foretell (to):	prever
get into sth (to):	meter-se num assunto
guide (to):	guiar
in advance:	com antecedência
living:	vivo
make certain (to):	garantir
major:	importante
mention (to):	fazer referência a
move:	ação, passo
press conference:	coletiva (entrevista)
quickly:	rapidamente
séance:	sessão espírita
shortly after:	pouco depois
supress (to):	suprimir
warn (to):	avisar

Glossary

activity	atividade	benefit (to)	beneficiar-se
adventurous	aventureiro/a	big-hearted	de grande coração
alone	sozinho/a	body	corpo
alternative	alternativa	bossy	mandão/ona
appreciate (to)	apreciar, valorizar	both	ambos/as
back	de novo, outra vez	business	negócio
balanced	equilibrado	calm	tranquilo/a

careful	cuidadoso/a
cause (to)	causar
chance	oportunidade
charming	encantador/a
classical	clássico/a, tradicional
clearly	claramente
confident	seguro/a, confiante
cool	frio/a, sereno/a
develop (to)	desenvolver
direct	direto/a
dislike (to)	não gostar de
discuss (to)	debater
enjoy (to)	desfrutar (curtir)
easy	fácil
environment	ambiente
enthusiastic	entusiasta
equipment	equipamento, máquina
even	inclusive
fantasy	fantasia
fantasize (to)	fantasiar
feel (to)	sentir, sentir-se
financial	financeiro
find (to)	encontrar
focus on (to)	focar em
free	livre
friction	fricção
get involved (to)	envolver-se
gift	presente
harmony	harmonia
honest	honesto/a
however	entretanto
idealistic	idealista
improve (to)	melhorar
instead	em vez de, em lugar de
instinctive	instintivo/a
intend (to)	ter a intenção de
jealous	ciumento/a
judgement	juízo
just	justo
leader	líder
leadership	liderança
look	olhada
malfunction (to)	funcionar mal
make a decision (to)	tomar uma decisão
maybe	talvez
motivated	motivado/a
needs	necessidades
on your mind	em mente
open	aberto/a
optimistic	otimista
over	ao longo de
overemotional	muito emotivo/a
peacefully	pacificamente
passionate	apaixonado/a
patient	paciente
piece	pedaço
partner	casal / companheiro/a
playful	brincalhão
point of view	ponto de vista
pompous	pomposo/a, ostentoso/a
private	privado, particular
question	assunto, pergunta
quiet	tranquilo/a, silencioso/a
really	realmente
relationship	relação, relacionamento
responsible	responsável
regret (to)	arrepender-se
romance	amor, romance
safe	seguro/a
secretive	reservado/a, calado/a
sensitive	sensível
sides	lados
skill	habilidade
special	especial
spend (to)	gastar (tempo ou dinheiro)
spirit	espírito
stable	estável
stubborn	teimoso/a
take part in (to)	participar
tend to (to)	tender a
think (to)	pensar
trusting	confiante
try (to)	tentar
uncompleted	inacabado/a
unemotional	desapaixonado/a
unpredictable	essencial
value (to)	valorizar
warm	morno, afetuoso/a (fig.)
weekly	semanalmente

Transcript

Juliet: And now it's time for our weekly look at horoscopes. By the way, Sue, do you believe in horoscopes?
Sue: Well, I love horoscopes.
J: Stuart?
Stuart: No, not really.
J: What about you, Brian? Do you believe in them?
Brian: Not much, no.
J: Well I do. Now, let's start with **Aquarius**. Aquarius, you are imaginative and unpredictable. You have an independent personality but you tend to be cool and unemotional, which is good in business, but can make personal relationships difficult. This week, you'll try to make everyone happy, but it won't be easy, so spend your time only on the people who will appreciate you. Romance is a big possibility this week.
St: Pisces, you are generous but you often fantasize instead of focusing on the real world. You are sensitive to your partner's needs, but tend to be secretive about your needs. This week, technology will cause you some real problems. Important pieces of equipment will malfunction just when you need them, so do things in the simplest way possible.
S: Aries, you are open, energetic, and dynamic. You are ambitious but you can be impulsive. In the next few days, life will get better financially, maybe with a gift, or the chance to get some extra money. You'll feel very responsible, but don't get involved in the financial problems of other people. Stay calm.
B: Taurus, you like a safe, stable environment where you can live peacefully and happily. You can be quite stubborn and possessive, but you value family and live for the people you love. In the next week, a lot of people around you will express different opinions to yours, so it'll be a good week for listening to other points of view.
J: Gemini, you are energetic, adventurous and inventive. You are involved in a lot of different things, but sometimes leave them uncompleted. Over the next week, philosophical and religious questions will be on your mind, but don't be dogmatic when you discuss things. Even if you don't intend to offend someone, you probably will.
St: Cancer, you are trusting and private. You tend to be protective and overemotional. In the next few days, your focus will be on your home, and to be alone, but you'll want to take part in social activities. Try to do both! Today plan time with others, and also try to find someplace quiet where you can spend an hour alone.
S: Leo, you are enthusiastic and playful. You are also confident, but warm and big-hearted at the same time. You enjoy being the leader, and being the centre of attention, but can be pompous and bossy. In the next few days you'll feel your best, so you'll benefit by spending more time socialising. Go to a party, meet people, you won't regret it.
B: Virgo, you're good in teams and you enjoy helping others. However, your perfectionism makes you focus on small details in relationships. And that can cause friction with

your partner. During the next week, don't try to do too many things at the same time – you'll only have problems. Your leadership skills will also be very strong, so lead others by your example.

J: **Libra**, you are charming and you love harmony. You like things balanced and you consider the alternatives when making decisions because you tend to see both sides of an argument. In the next week you'll tend to analyze your options too much, and that will cause problems if you're not careful. The simple solution is to make decisions more quickly, especially on small questions.

St: **Scorpio**, you are adaptable and instinctive, philosophical and intense, but relationships with Scorpios are never easy, because you can be jealous and secretive. In the next week you'll feel that others don't understand you. If you communicate well, the transformation will be dramatic. Your judgement about money won't be very good, but don't worry, next week things will be back to normal.

S: **Sagittarius**, you are honest, idealistic, and optimistic. You tend to see the big picture, not just the small details. You have a free spirit and want to experience everything but you tend to be too direct, and that can cause friction. In the next week, you'll want to spend more time with someone special. Your relationships will improve and develop. It'll be a good week for romance.

B: And finally: **Capricorn**, you are patient, responsible and motivated. You want to "make things work". In romance you are classical and passionate but you tend to dislike fantasy. The next week will not be a good time to make important decisions about your future because you won't be thinking clearly enough. Instead, focus on your health; it will be a good week for your body.

J: And that's all for this week.

TRACK 10 / CD 1 ▶▶ QUIZ SHOW

LISTENING

1 Ouça a faixa e tente responder você mesmo as 10 perguntas do **quiz**. Recomendamos que se dê uma pausa depois de cada pergunta.

1.	6.
2.	7.
3.	8.
4.	9.
5.	10.

2 Quem dá a resposta correta: a) **Brian**, b) **Juliet**, c) **Sue**, d) **Stuart** or e) **nobody**? Indique em cada caso.

1. Which country has the best environmental policy in the world?
2. Which country has the highest cost of living?
3. Which country has the lowest cost of living?
4. Which is the biggest island in the Mediterranean?
5. Which country has the highest beer consumption per capita?
6. Which country has the biggest wine consumption per capita?
7. Which is the world's busiest airport in terms of passengers?
8. Which country has the highest life expectancy for women?
9. Which country has the highest life expectancy for men?
10. Which football club is the most successful in European competitions?

3 Do ponto de vista da posição da sílaba tônica, coloque os nomes dos países e das ilhas abaixo na coluna correspondente.

> Australia · Cyprus · Finland · France · Germany · Iceland · Iran · Italy · Japan
> Majorca · (New) Zealand · Norway · Pakistan · Paraguay · (The) Philippines
> Portugal · Sardinia · Spain · Sweden · Switzerland · Venezuela

One-syllable names	Stress on first syllable	Stress on second syllable	Stress on third syllable
France	Cyprus	Australia	

VOCABULARY

4 Dê o antônimo de cada adjetivo.

> uncompetitive · low · quiet · small · expensive · slow · mean · bad

big / large _____ busy _____
cheap _____ competitive _____
good _____ high _____
generous _____ quick _____

5 Complete as frases abaixo com um dos adjetivos vistos.

1. Generally speaking, South American economies are not considered very _____ by experts.
2. Restaurants are usually quite _____ on Friday and Saturdays evenings.
3. I wanted to go by train, but it wasn't especially _____; only € 10 less than flying.
4. She gave me a really _____ bottle of whisky for my birthday. It was so _____ of her.
5. Let's not go out tonight; I'd like to have a _____ night at home.
6. Hotel prices are generally _____ in summer and _____ in winter, on the coast anyway.
7. In Brazil the stereotypical Arab descendent is a _____ character.
8. This letter took four days to get from Australia to Britain - that was really _____ !

Ordinal numbers

Os numerais ordinais são formados a partir do numeral cardinal, ao qual se acrescenta a terminação **-th**: **seven ▶ seventh**, **ten ▶ tenth**, MAS **five ▶ fifth**. As exceções são **one ▶ first**, **two ▶ second**, **three ▶ third**. Portanto, diríamos: **December the twenty first, the second of October, the third of November**. As datas também podem ser escritas com números, como em português: **21/12, 02/10, 03/11**. Atenção! No inglês americano primeiro vem o mês, depois o dia: **12/21, 10/02, 11/03**. Logo, **06/07** equivaleria a **July 6th** em inglês britânico e a **June 7th** nos Estados Unidos.

6 Escreva as datas abaixo em forma de números, em inglês britânico (a) e norte-americano (b).

1. The thirty first of October a) ____ b) ____
2. May the first a) ____ b) ____
3. The 20th of November, 1975 a) ____ b) ____
4. The fifteenth of August a) ____ b) ____
5. December 6th a) ____ b) ____
6. 24th October, 1929 a) ____ b) ____
7. July 4th a) ____ b) ____
8. September 11th, 2001 a) ____ b) ____

GRAMMAR

Superlatives

7 Coloque estes adjetivos na coluna correspondente.

> big · busy · cheap · competitive · expensive · good · high
> generous · large · low · quick

One syllable adjectives	Two syllable adjectives	Three (+) syllable adjectives

8 Leia a transcrição prestando atenção sobretudo nas formas superlativas. Em seguida, complete as regras de formação do superlativo.

For **good** and **bad**, the superlatives are **the best** and **the worst**.
- For other adjectives with one syllable, we put ▓▓▓▓ before the adjective, and add ▓▓▓▓ to the base form of the adjective.
- For adjectives with two syllables that end with the letter ▓▓▓▓ we put ▓▓▓▓ before the adjective, and add ▓▓▓▓ to the base form of the adjective.
- For most adjectives with two syllables, we put ▓▓▓▓ and ▓▓▓▓ before the adjective
- For all adjectives with three or more syllables, we put ▓▓▓▓ and ▓▓▓▓ before the adjective.

9 Complete com o superlativo que falta. Depois, assinale a resposta correta.

1. Which is ▓▓▓▓ **(large)** city in Europe in terms of population?
   ▓ a) London ▓ b) Paris ▓ c) Milan ▓ d) Moscow

2. Which country is ▓▓▓▓ **(generous)** in foreign aid?
   ▓ a) Norway ▓ b) Denmark ▓ c) Netherlands ▓ d) Saudi Arabia

3. Which country has ▓▓▓▓ **(competitive)** economy?
   ▓ a) The USA ▓ b) Singapore ▓ c) Australia ▓ d) Canada

What or Which?

Usamos **which** quando as opções de resposta são limitadas (**Which bag is yours?**) e **what** quando a pergunta é do tipo aberta (**What's your name?**).

10 Complete este diálogo, que se passa em um restaurante, com **which** ou **what**.

- ▓▓▓▓ have you got for dessert?
- We've got ice-cream.
- ▓▓▓▓ flavours have you got?
- We've got banana and stracciatella. ▓▓▓▓ one would you like?
- Straciatella? ▓▓▓▓ is straciatella?
- It's an Italian ice-cream, basically it's vanilla with bits of chocolate in it.
- Okay, I'll have that, thanks.

Take-away English

Come on!	Venha! / Vamos!
the Med	o Mediterrâneo
You're right.	Você tem razão.
Go on!	Continue!
Well done!	Está benfeito!
(to) get the right answer	acertar a resposta
(to) take something into account	levar algo em consideração

CULTURAL note

Making a countable noun plural in modern English is easy. We simply add an **s**: **minute** ▶ **minutes**, or **–ies** to a noun that finishes with **y**: **party** ▶ **parties**, and **–es** to a noun that finishes with an **o**: **hero** ▶ **heroes**. But it wasn't always this easy. In old Anglo-Saxon, plurals were made by adding **–en** or **–ee** to the singular, and the definite article changed too, but in the 10th century this complex grammar started to become simpler when Vikings colonisers and native Anglo-Saxons began to mix and had to understand each other's language. Only a few words in modern English maintain their old Anglo-Saxon plural forms: **child** ▶ **children**, **woman** ▶ **women**, **man** ▶ **men**, and **foot** ▶ **feet**, **tooth** ▶ **teeth**, **mouse** ▶ **mice** are the most important ones.

Glossary

air	ar	island	ilha
airport	aeroporto	litre	litro
answer	resposta	men	homens
beer	cerveja	opposite	contrário, oposto
biodiversity	biodiversidade	passenger	passageiro/a
called	chamado	policy	política
choice	opção, escolha	public health	saúde pública
citizen	cidadão/ã	quality	qualidade
consider (to)	considerar, levar em consideração	question	pergunta
		ready	pronto, preparado
consumption	consumo	resources	recursos
cost of living	custo de vida	right	correto, certo
country	país	social security	seguridade social
energy	energia	start (to)	começar, iniciar
environmental	meio ambiente	successful	bem-sucedido/a
expensive	caro/a	surprise	surpresa
flight	voo	sustainable	sustentável
life expectancy	expectativa de vida	think (to)	crer, pensar
get (to)	obter	water	água
health	saúde	wine	vinho
index	índice	women	mulheres
in fact	de fato	world	mundo

Transcript

Stuart: And now it's quiz time. Has everyone got their questions ready?
All: Yeah.
St: Let's see who can get the right answer the quickest. Is everyone ready?
All: Yeah.
Sue: Ok, I'll start. Which country has the best environmental policy in the world?
Juliet: What do you mean?
S: Well, this is an international index that considers air quality, water resources, biodiversity and habitat, natural resources, and sustainable energy.
J: Okay, and what are the options?
S: a) the Czech Republic, b) Finland, c) New Zealand and d) Sweden.
J: I'd say Finland.
St: And I think it's New Zealand.
S: You're right. That's one to Stuart.
St: Okay, my question: Which country has the highest cost of living?
J: The highest cost of living?
St: Yeah, when everything is taken into account, which is the most expensive country to live in? And the options are: a) France, b) Japan, c) Norway, and d) Switzerland.
Brian: Is it Switzerland?
St: No, it isn't Switzerland.
J: Is it Japan?
St: No, not Japan.
S: I think Norway is more expensive than France, so I'll say Norway.
St: You're right. Can I ask another question?
All: Oh, go on then.
St: Right, this is the opposite: Which country has the lowest cost of living? The lowest cost of living. Your options are: a) Iran, b) The Philippines, c) Pakistan, d) Paraguay.
J: The cheapest country to live in?
St: Yeah, more or less.
B: I think Iran is probably less expensive to live in than the others, so I would say that, Iran.
St: That's right! Iran has the lowest cost of living in the world. One point to Brian.
B: Okay, here's my question. Are you ready? Which is the biggest island in the Mediterranean sea? The biggest island in the Mediterranean. The options are: a) Cyprus, b) Mallorca, c) Sardinia and d) Sicily.
St: I think I know that one – it's Cyprus.
S: No, I think Sicily is bigger than Cyprus.
B: Well Stuart's wrong and Sue's right. Sicily is in fact the biggest island in the Med. Well done. Your question, Sue.
S: Well I've got two more questions, and they're both about alcohol. First, which country has the highest beer consumption per capita?
B: The place where people drink the most beer?
S: Per capita, yes.
St: Okay, what are the choices?
S: Okay, your options are 1) Australia 2) the Czech Republic, 3) Germany or 4) Venezuela.
St: Venezuela?
B: Well that's a surprise. Anyway, I think I'd say Australia.
J: I think it's the Czech Republic.
S: You're right, Juliet. How did you know?
J: Because it's got *pub* in the name, Re-pub-lic.
All: Come on Jules!
S: Well in fact beer consumption is higher in Germany than Australia, but Venezuela is still the third highest in the world, Stuart, after the Czech Republic and Germany.
B: I didn't know that.

S: Apparently the average Czech citizen drinks 81.7 litres of beer a year.
J: Amazing.
St: Wow, now can we have your second question, Sue?
S: Of course, it's basically the same, but this time it's wine consumption, so – which country has the biggest wine consumption per capita? Your choices are: 1) France, 2) Italy, 3) Portugal, and 4) Switzerland.
B: Italy!
J: No, they drink more wine in France than in Italy, Brian.
B: I think they drink less in France–
S: Well you're right and wrong. Brian. France is fourth and Italy is third.
St: So it must be Portugal.
S: Exactly, 31.5 litres per person per year. And Switzerland is second.
J: Switzerland? That's incredible.
B: Especially for wine.
S: Yeah, yeah, amazing.
St: Okay, my question again. This one is about airports. Which is the world's busiest airport in terms of passengers?
J: In terms of number of passengers?
S: Not the number of flights?
St: Right. Here are your options: a) London *Heathrow*, b) Tokyo *Haneda*, c) Atlanta *Hartsfield*, and d) Chicago *O'Hare*.
S: Chicago – what's it called – O'Hare?
J: Heathrow.
B: I'll say Tokyo.
St: Well you're all wrong – Atlanta Hartsfield is the world's busiest airport.
J: I was sure it was Heathrow.
St: Heathrow is the busiest airport in Europe in terms of passengers, and I think Paris *Charles de Gaulle* has the most flights.
J: The biggest number of flights?
St: Yeah – it's busier than Heathrow when it comes to the number of flights. Okay, here's another question: Which country has the highest life expectancy for women?
S: For women?
St: Yes, in which country do women – statistically speaking – live the longest? a) Hong Kong, b) Japan, c) Spain, d) Switzerland.
J: It must be Switzerland –
S: Because they drink the most wine?
J: Yes.
B: I think it's Spain.
S: And I'd say Japan.
St: Why do you say Japan, Sue?
S: Oh, I think because the Japanese have one of the best diets, they have one of the best public health and social security systems.
St: Well, you're right, Japan is the correct answer. 86.4 years is the average there.
S: Wow, that's a lot.
B: And what about for men?
St: All right, which country has the highest life expectancy for men? a) Iceland, b) Hong Kong, c) Japan, d) Sweden.
S: I'd say Japan again.
B: Iceland.
J: For me, Sweden.
St: It's Iceland in fact. 79.5 years.
J: That's strange isn't it? Because women usually live longer than men.
S: Except in Iceland!
St: No, in fact, In Iceland men *don't* live as long as women; women there have a life expectancy of 83.2 years.
B: Ok. My question. It's about football. Which football club is the most successful in European competitions?
J: No idea.
B: Come on, Juliet. Try: a) Real Madrid, b) AC Milan, c) Bayern Munich, d) Manchester United.
J: Real Madrid? –
B: – is the correct answer.

TRACK 11 / CD 1 ▶▶ THE SOUL OF A MAN

LISTENING

1 True or false?

	true	false
1. Connor wants to hear a song called *The song of a man*.		
2. Stuart saw the Martin Scorsese film too.		
3. Most of the first blues singers were women.		
4. Blues had a small audience in the USA.		
5. Blues was very influential on British music in the 1970s.		

2 Assinale a opção correta.

1. The title of the Martin Scorsese film and the Willie Johnson song are **different / the same**.
2. Blind Willie Johnson wrote the song in **1930 / 1931**.
3. The Blues originated in the Mississippi Delta in the early **19th / 20th** century.
4. **Hillbilly / Race music** was the name given to music for black audiences.
5. British musicians made the blues more **electric / acoustic**.

VOCABULARY

Like

S: And then suddenly it got discovered by young white musicians in England.
C: Yeah, people **like** John Mayall, Steve Winwood, Jimmy Page, Eric Clapton.

A preposição **like** ("como") é muito utilizada em inglês, até mais do que o verbo **like** ("gostar").

Cuajada is a bit **like** yoghurt.   *Coalhada é quase como iogurte.*
You're starting to talk **like** your mother.   *Você está começando a falar como sua mãe.*

3 Indique se nas sentenças abaixo **like** é um verbo ou uma preposição.

	verb	prep.
1. He runs **like** the wind.		
2. I **like** you, Nathan, but I don't want to marry you.		
3. She didn't **like** the film very much.		
4. She looks **like** her mother.		
5. When did you start to wear your hair **like** that?		
6. Do you **like** Thai food?		
7. In some countries, **like** Australia, people have to vote in a general election.		
8. She doesn't **like** getting up early in the morning.		
9. In the final against Brazil, they played **like** giants.		
10. On Saturday morning, we **like** going to the market to do the shopping.		

Nos Estados Unidos, usa-se **like** antes de adjetivos, de exclamações ou de perguntas. Embora gramaticalmente não seja considerado correto, tal emprego ocorre na linguagem coloquial.

I was **like** terrified.
She was **like** *What!*
We were **like** *What are you doing here*?

GRAMMAR

Noun formation

Os substantivos em inglês se dividem em várias categorias.

abstract nouns: love, hate, peace, history...
proper nouns or names: Edward, Buenos Aires, Lancaster University...
general nouns: countable (photo/s, camera/s, euro/s, CD/s...)
　　　　　　　　uncountable (music, water, bread, work...)

A partir dos adjetivos, podemos criar substantivos.

real (adjective) ▶ **realism** (noun: thing) ▶ **realist** (noun: person)
surreal (adjective) ▶ **surrealism** (noun: thing) ▶ **surrealist** (noun: person)
optimistic (adjective) ▶ **optimism** (noun: thing) ▶ **optimist** (noun: person)

Atenção! Os sufixos **-ism** e **-ist** são muito habituais, mas não são os únicos.

4 Ouça ou consulte a transcrição e escreva o substantivo correspondente aos adjetivos abaixo.

adjectives	noun
sad	
lonely	

Da mesma forma, quais são os substantivos de **happy**, **black**, **small**, **dark**, **late** e **great**? Escreva-os em seu caderno.

5 A partir dos verbos podemos criar substantivos. Escreva no lugar correspondente os substantivos dos verbos abaixo.

verb	noun (with -tion)	noun (with -sion)
(to) classify		
(to) transform		
(to) invade		

6 Com o prefixo **in-** formamos substantivos negativos. Complete o quadro.

noun	negative / opposite noun
justice	

Agora, escreva em seu caderno os antônimos dos adjetivos abaixo.

> capability · coherence · compatibility · consistency · convenience
> dependence · dignity · discretion · subordination

Question tags

Stuart admite que Connor já conhece uma informação e usa uma **question tag (didn't it?)**: and it became very popular in England, **didn't it?** As **question tags** representam 25% das perguntas que se formulam no inglês oral. Equivalem ao que utilizamos em português quando acabamos uma frase dizendo "não?" / "né?" / "não é verdade?".

7 Relacione cada frase com sua respectiva **question tag**. Em seguida, escute e comprove.

> wasn't it? (2) · was it? · didn't it? (3) · were they? · aren't you? · don't you, Connor?

1. You're **calling** about the blues, _____
2. And the film **had** the same title, _____
3. It **was recorded** in 1930, _____
4. You probably **know**, _____
5. The most important early blues singers **weren't** men, _____
6. And it was the blues that **led** to rock and roll, _____
7. ... which until then **was played** mostly on acoustic guitars, _____
8. ... it **wasn't played** on most of the radio stations, _____
9. ... and it **became** very popular in England, _____

8 Complete a regra das **question tags** com as seguintes palavras.

> affirmative · affirmative · negative · negative · question · **do** · an auxiliary verb

The main part of the sentence does not have the word order of a (1) _____ . The tag is formed with (2) _____ . If there is one in the first part of the sentence, we use it for the tag. If there isn't one, we use the verb (3) _____ in the appropriate verb tense. If the main part of the sentence is (4) _____ , the tag is (5) _____ . If the main part of the sentence is (6) _____ , the tag is (7) _____ .

9 Agora, escreva a **question tag** para cada frase.

1. Flamengo's from Rio de Janeiro, _____ ?
2. This was made in Malaysia, _____ ?
3. You didn't like the music, _____ ?
4. He smokes, _____ ?
5. You're French, _____ ?
6. That's an interesting opinion, _____ ?
7. When you said you studied Philosophy, that wasn't true, _____ ?
8. I think we need to have a coffee break, _____ ?
9. You can't speak Arabic, _____ ?
10. We saw something very similar in Berlin, _____ ?

10 Ouça as frases abaixo no CD. Veja como são pronunciadas as **question tags**. Como é a entonação: ascendente ou descendente?

1. You're calling about the blues, **aren't you?**
2. And the film had the same title, **didn't it?**
3. It was recorded in 1930, **wasn't it?**
4. It wasn't played on most of the radio stations, **was it?**

Past passive

Na faixa, Connor utiliza a voz passiva: **It was written in 1930 and (was) recorded in 1931**. A passiva se forma com o verbo **to be** (no tempo verbal correspondente) seguido do **past participle** do verbo principal. A forma é similar à da passiva em português: A principal diferença é que em inglês talvez se use mais.

> Voz ativa: Picasso **painted** Guernica in 1937.
> Voz passiva: Guernica **was painted** by Picasso in 1937.

A passiva pode ser empregada tanto com o **past simple** quanto com os outros tempos verbais. Vejamos alguns exemplos:

Experts consider that the face and hands **were painted** by Rembrandt. *(past)*
The new airport **will be opened** by the Prime Minister. *(future)*
These cars **are made** near Detroit. *(present simple)*
A new contract **is being negotiated** between the club and the players.
(present continuous)

Connor diz **It was written in 1930...** porque já sabemos que Blind Willie Johnson compôs a música, e diz **(it was) recorded in 1931** porque já conhecemos o nome do artista e queremos enfatizar o ano da gravação.

Na linguagem coloquial, pode-se usar **got** (em vez de **be**) + **past participle**.

... in the 1960s suddenly it **got discovered** – or rediscovered – by young white musicians in England (...) it was virtually dead in the USA, but then **got revitalised** in England.

Volte a ler as frases e note que é empregado **by** para introduzir a pessoa que realiza a ação.

... in the 1960s suddenly it got discovered – or rediscovered – **by** young white musicians in England...

11 Passe as frases abaixo para a voz passiva.

1. Giuseppe Verdi wrote this opera in 1871.

2. The fire destroyed five houses.

3. The President of the USA will open the conference.

4. We are destroying the ozone layer.

5. Lewis Hamilton won the 2008 Formula 1 world championship.

6. *The Mail* published photos of Madonna's wedding to Guy Ritchie.

7. People criticised the United Nations for not preventing the massacre of civilians.

8. Antoni Gaudí designed the Sagrada Familia.

9. They make some excellent wine in Chile.

10. Visitors to the event drank 5,000 litres of beer.

Might

Stuart diz: **Some of our listeners might not know why this kind of music is called the blues**. **Might** é um verbo auxiliar modalizador que serve para expressar possibilidade. Deve ser seguido do infinitivo sem **to**: **Juliet might like some more wine, I think**. / **That might not be the best solution**.

CULTURAL note

Where and when did the blues begin? Most people believe that it was in the Mississippi Delta in the late 19th century, and that the first blues song was *Memphis Blues*, written by W.C. Handy in 1906. Blues songs were often sung in a style more like rhythmic talk than melody. The singer talked about his or her personal problems in a difficult world: **poverty**, hard physical work, prison, **lost love**, racism, violence, the **cruelty** of the police, and oppression by white people in the South, **suffering** in its many forms, and blue is another word for melancholy.

In the 1930s to the 1950s blues gained a **larger** public in other parts of the USA, but it was still very much a minority form of music. J. B. Lenoir from Chicago recorded several LPs using acoustic guitar. One of the greats, his songs commented on political **issues** like racism in the South or the Vietnam War.

In the 1950s, Chicago blues artists like Muddy Waters were the first to use electric instruments, making the sound heavier.

In the 1960s there was a blues boom in England, when British blues artists like Eric Clapton and Cream, John Mayall, the Rolling Sones, and the Yardbirds electrified the blues, reviving it when it was becoming less popular in America. But at the same time Texas blues artists like T-Bone Walker started to include elements of rock and roll, and Detroit blues artists like John Lee Hooker used electric guitars and a wider **range** of instruments. By the end of the 1960s, the blues was beginning to have an enormous influence on **mainstream** popular and rock music, from Jimi Hendrix to Led Zeppelin.

Glossary
cruelty: crueldade
issue: questão
larger: maior
lost love: amor perdido
mainstream: de sucesso popular *(fig.)*
poverty: pobreza
range: gama, variedade
suffering: sofrimento

Take-away English

*Almost nobody knew it existed.	Quase ninguém sabia que existia.
by the early 60s	no início dos anos 1960
I am afraid...	Estou com receio de que...
You certainly know your history.	Você certamente conhece sua história.

*Com **almost nobody** emprega-se o verbo afirmativo.

Glossary

actually	na verdade	minority	minoria
audience	público	of course	(é) claro
basically	basicamente	originate (to)	iniciar, ter sua origem
black	negro/a	outside	fora
blind	cego/a	poor (the)	os pobres
certainly	certamente	popular	popular, conhecido
early	princípio	probably	provavelmente
emotion	emoção	recording	gravação
enormous	enorme	rediscover	redescobrir
especially	especialmente	request	pedido, solicitação
experience	experiência	revitalise (to)	revitalizar, estimular
fascinating	fascinante	sadness	tristeza
go ahead!	vá em frente!	send back (to)	devolver
great	ótimo, excelente	singer	cantor/a
happen (to)	passar, ocorrer	small	pequeno/a
hear (to)	ouvir	station	(a) radio, estação
influence (to)	influenciar	style	estilo
injustice	injustiça	suddenly	de repente
interesting	interessante	title	título
invasion	invasão	until	até
listener	ouvinte	virtually	praticamente
loneliness	solidão	white	branco/a
melancholy	melancolia		

Transcript

Stuart: And it's time for another music request. Go ahead, Connor.
Connor: Hello, Stuart?
S: You're calling about the blues, aren't you?
C: That's right.
S: And what song would you like to hear?
C: I'd like to hear an old blues song, by a singer called Blind Willie Johnson and it's called *The Soul of a Man*.
S: And why that particular song, Connor?
C: Well, it was in an excellent TV film about the blues, by Martin Scorsese a few years ago.
S: Ah yes, I saw that. It was really great. And the film had the same title, didn't it?
C: Yeah, that's right. And even though the recording quality of the song isn't very good, there's so much emotion in it.
S: That's right; it was recorded in 1930, wasn't it?
C: Almost, it was written in 1930 and recorded in 1931.
S: Well you certainly know your history, Connor.
C: I'm a fan of the blues.
S: Some of our listeners might not

know why this kind of music is called *the blues*. You probably know, don't you, Connor?
C: Yes, it's because blue is the colour of – er – melancholy, and basically the blues is about sadness, and loneliness and injustice.
S: Yes, the blues was born basically in the Mississippi Delta in the early years of the twentieth century. And it was the music of the poor –
C: But especially the black poor – and the most important early blues singers weren't men, were they?
S: No, I didn't know that actually –
C: Yeah, they were mainly women.
S: Is that right?
C: Yes, it wasn't until the 1920s that men singers became popular.
S: That's interesting.
C: And at first the music recording industry had a classification of what they called *race music*.
S: What do you mean?
C: Yeah, I mean the music they sold to white audiences was called *hillbilly music*, and the music they sold to the black audience was called *race music*.
S: Race music? God! You know, I think one of the fascinating things about twentieth century music is that so many musical styles originated in the experience of the black poor in the South of the USA. The blues, of course –
C: And it was the blues that led to rock and roll, didn't it?
S: True, but not only the blues. Jazz has the same southern black origins, and gospel too. But the blues was always very much a minority music, with a very small audience. Outside America almost nobody knew it existed. In the USA it wasn't played on most of the radio stations, was it?
C: No, no way.
S: And it certainly wasn't on TV. And then in the 1960s suddenly it got discovered – or rediscovered – by young white musicians in England.
C: Yeah, people like John Mayall, Steve Winwood, Jimmy Page, Eric Clapton-
S: That's right, and they electrified the blues, which until then was played mostly on acoustic guitars, wasn't it? **C:** Yeah.
S: And they transformed it, and it became very popular in England, didn't it?
C: Yeah.
S: And was sent back across the Atlantic. Then suddenly the blues got a much bigger audience in the USA.
C: And in England in the late 60s it had an enormous influence on people like the first Fleetwood Mac, and of course Led Zeppelin they were very influenced by the blues. And Jimmy Hendrix too. And the Rolling Stones of course.
S: Of course, the Stones. And in fact a similar transformation happened with rock and roll. By the early 1960s it was virtually dead in the USA.
C: That's right.
S: But then got revitalised in England, and there was a British invasion of popular music in north America in the mid 60s. But anyway, I'd like to talk about this all night, but we haven't got time I'm afraid, Connor,
C: Sure.
S: So thanks a lot for your call, and here's your song.
C: Thanks a lot, Stuart.

TRACK 12 / CD 1 ▶▶ SELLING PHONE IN

LISTENING

1 Relacione o texto com as fotos.

1 2 3 4 5

6 7 8 9 10

- an adult's bike
- a stereo
- a motorbike
- a mobile phone
- an electric guitar
- a home studio
- a laptop computer
- a kid's bike
- an acoustic guitar
- a cat with kittens

2 Escute e complete o quadro com algumas das informações abaixo.

Things for sale: two adult's bikes · two kid's bikes · a motorbike · a stereo
a home studio · an acoustic guitar · an electric guitar · a laptop computer
a mobile phone · four kittens / **Price:** nothing · € 40 · € 50 · € 100 · € 400
€ 500 for one · € 750 · € 800 for two · € 850 · € 1000

	things for sale	price
Caller 1		
Caller 2		
Caller 3		
Caller 4		
Caller 5		

3 Responda às perguntas de cada produto abaixo.

1. Product	Does it work well?	Why is he selling it?	What's his phone number?
2. Product	How old?	Why is he selling it?	What's his phone number?
3. Thing	Colour	Why is he giving them away?	What's his email?
4. Product	Description	Why is he selling it?	What's his phone number?
5. Products	Are they hers?	Why is she selling them?	What's her email?

4 Escute com atenção as frases abaixo. Atente especialmente aos auxiliares **be**, em **to**, **for** e no pronome **them**. Marque as sílabas e as palavras que são pronunciadas com mais ênfase. Depois, repita-as em voz alta, imitando a entonação.

1. ... so I'm trying to sell this one now.
2. How much are you asking for it?
3. Right, that's Steve, who's selling a laptop computer and he's asking € 400 for it.
4. Why are you selling them, if I can ask?
5. Go ahead, Chris, what are you trying to sell?

VOCABULARY

Buy and sell

Esta unidade fala de vender (**sell**), de comprar (**buy**) e de presentear (**give away**) coisas. Os três verbos são irregulares: **buy ▶ bought ▶ bought, sell ▶ sold ▶ sold, give away ▶ gave away ▶ given away**.

5 Complete a conversação abaixo, que se passa em uma loja, com a forma correta dos verbos anteriores.

Customer: Hello, I'm having some problems with this mobile phone that I .... here last month.
Shop: Right. Could I just see the **receipt** please?
Customer: It came with a special offer. € 100 of phone credit free.
Shop: That's strange. We don't usually .... that much credit.
Customer: Well, the shop assistant who .... it to me was very clear about that, € 100 free credit.
Shop: Let's have a look at the receipt - oh, you didn't .... the phone here, madam.
Customer: Yes I did. I always .... phones and computer **stuff** here. I'm sure I .... it here last month, as I told you.
Shop: Well, in the first place, we don't .... this model. And the receipt - if you look here - is from another shop.
Customer: Oh, maybe my boyfriend .... it for me, and told me the wrong name.
Shop: I'm sure.

receipt: recibo
stuff: coisas

Back

Keith diz: **We're moving back to Scotland** ("Vamos voltar à Escócia"). **Back** é uma partícula muito habitual. É empregada em combinação com muitos verbos e tem um significado parecido com **again**.

Às vezes expressa o retorno a um lugar ou um movimento em direção oposta.
I'll buy some flowers on my way **back** home.

Pode referir-se a um tempo passado:

Back in the 1970s we only had two or three TV channels.

Também expressa uma resposta ou uma repetição ("voltar a").

We wrote to you but you never wrote **back**.

Back se combina com preposições para formar **phrasal verbs**; os mais comuns são **back up** ("dar respaldo, "apoiar") e **back down** ("ficar para trás", "ser ultrapassado").

Try

Steve diz **I'm trying to sell a laptop**. **Try** ("tentar") é muito usado em inglês.

I'm **trying** to lose weight, but it's not easy if you have a social life.
We **tried** to get tickets for the concert, but we were too late.

É muito empregado no imperativo seguido de **to** ou **and**, e combinado com **will**.

Try and eat something – you'll feel a lot better if you do.

Também combina com preposições para formar **phrasal verbs**; os mais habituais são **try on** ("provar (uma roupa)") e **try out** ("pôr à prova").

Equipment

Barbara diz **an electric guitar and some studio recording equipment**. **Equipment** ("aparelho") é um substantivo incontável. Pronuncia-se /ekqwipment/.

- Is there a shop near here that sells skiing **equipment**?
- Yes, there's one near the river that has all kinds of sports **equipment**.

Contact

Steve diz: **You can contact me on 666 54 99 49**. Embora o verbo **contact** não peça preposição alguma, geralmente a informação que vem depois é que cobra a presença de uma.

Please **contact** me **at** home if necessary.

Cell or mobile?

Suzanne é norte-americana, por isso, diz **cell phone**. Também se usa **cell phone** no Canadá, Austrália e Nova Zelândia. Keith, por outro lado, diz **mobile phone**, expressão utilizada na Grã-Bretanha.

GRAMMAR

Present continuous

Juliet diz: **Why are you selling them?** Este tempo verbal se chama **present continuous** ou **present progressive**. E é formado com o verbo **be** + a forma em **-ing** do verbo principal.

6 Você sabe quando é que se usa esse tempo verbal? Assinale a opção correta.

We use the present continuous for something that is:
▪ happening now, as we speak ▪ always true ▪ possibly true in the future

Quantos exemplos deste tempo verbal você consegue encontrar em cada diálogo? Escreva o número em cada caso.

▪ Dialogue 1 (Liam and Sue)   ▪ Dialogue 4 (Juliet and Keith)
▪ Dialogue 2 (Maria Elena and Juliet) ▪ Dialogue 5 (Barbara and Sue)
▪ Dialogue 3 (Chis and Sue)

7 Empregue o **present simple** ou o **present continuous**.
1. She .... (**wear**) a lovely black dress.
2. I'm afraid Sue can't talk at the moment – she .... (**have**) a shower.
3. Every year they .... (**go**) to their house on the coast in August.
4. "Where .... (**stay**)?" "Us? At the Goya Hotel, near the cathedral."
5. And it's half time at Wembley, where England .... (**lose**) 2-1 to Italy.
6. "Do you .... (**play**) a musical instrument?" "I can play the piano a bit."
7. Could you answer the door please? I .... (**watch**) TV.
8. I can't hear you very well! The train .... (**go**) though a tunnel.
9. We normally .... (**spend**) Christmas with my husband's family.
10. I .... (**go**) to bed at midnight from Monday to Thursday.

O **present continuous** também é empregado para acontecimentos ocorridos durante um período de tempo que engloba o momento atual, mas não necessariamente o instante presente (a), e para acontecimentos que ocorrerão em um momento concreto do futuro (b).

8 Indique qual dos dois usos (a ou b) exemplifica cada uma das frases abaixo.

1. **I'm seeing** my dentist on Thursday at 10.30.
2. **We're flying** to Saint Petersburg on the 27th.
3. Very few people **are buying** houses at present.
4. **She's wearing** a lot of second-hand clothes these days.
5. **I'm thinking** of studying Anthropology next year.
6. I can't meet you for lunch next Friday. **I'm getting** married that day!
7. Terrorist attacks **are getting** more and more common.
8. The Olympics **are becoming** more and more professional.
9. People **are drinking** much more these days.
10. I'll be late home tonight: **I'm meeting** John after work.

Take-away English

Go ahead!	Vá em frente!
What's wrong with it?	Qual o problema? O que há de errado?
Good luck (with selling it)	Boa sorte (com a venda)
Good for you!	Fico feliz por você!
Give us a call.	Ligue para nós.
Never mind.	Não importa.

Glossary

adult	adulto	change (to)	trocar
any more	já não	check (to)	checar
ask (to)	pedir	compose (to)	compor
belong (to)	pertencer	computer	computador
better	melhor	country	país
bicycle	bicicleta	each	cada (um)
birthday	aniversário	equipment	aparelho, equipamento
both	ambos/as	free	grátis, gratuito
caller	a pessoa que telefona	give away (to)	presentear
cat	gato/a	home	casa

kittens	filhotes (de gato)
laptop	laptop
latest	último, mais recente
leave (to)	deixar, sair
look after (to)	cuidar de, ocupar-se de
look to (to)	tentar
lovely	amável
move back (to)	voltar
offer (to)	oferecer
on air	no ar, ao vivo
pet	animal de estimação
place	lugar
recording equipment	gravador
sell (to)	vender
someone else	outra pessoa
space	espaço
take up (to)	ocupar (espaço)
things	coisas
try to (to)	tentar

Transcript

1

Juliet: Now what have we got, Sue?
Sue: We've got some callers who are trying to sell things.
J: So who's first?
S: Let's see. Our first caller is called Steve. Go ahead, caller!
Steve: Am I on air?
S: You sure are, Steve.
St: Okay, I'm trying to sell a laptop computer.
S: Why? What's wrong with it?
St: Nothing, it works perfectly, but someone gave me a new one for my 15th birthday, and it's better, so I'm trying to sell this one now.
S: Can you tell us about it?
St: Okay, it's a Sony 150 Gb, 12-inch screen and it works perfectly.
S: Thanks Steve. How much are you asking for it?
St: I'm asking € 400, and you can contact me on 666 54 99 49.
S: Okay, thanks for calling. Right, that's Steve, who's selling a laptop computer and he's asking € 400 for it. Call him on 666 54 99 49.

2

Juliet: Next we have Suzanne. Suzanne, are you there?
Suzanne: Sure I'm here. Hello!
J: Hello.
S: Okay, I'm looking to sell two bicycles, both in excellent condition –
J: Sorry Suzanne, are they kids' bikes or adults' bikes?
S: Oh, they're both adult bikes, just three years old, and I'm selling them for € 500 each or € 800 for both of them.
J: € 500 for one or € 800 for both? That's a good price. Why are you selling them, if I can ask?
S: Yeah. I just moved into a new apartment and the bikes are taking up too much space in the new place.
J: Okay Suzanne, and what do you want people to do if they're interested?
S: Call me of course, ha! My cell phone number is 647 50 50 71.
J: Thank you, Suzanne. She's offering two bicycles for € 800 or € 500 if you only want one of them, and her number is 647 50 50 71.

3

Sue: And our next caller is Chris. Go ahead, Chris, what are you trying to sell?
Chris: Nothing.
S: So why are you calling?
C: My cat had kittens last month and I'm giving away the kittens because I haven't got space for them at home.
S: So you're giving them away free?
S: Yes. There are four of them. And they're black and white, and very beautiful. And I want them to go a good home where someone will look after them. Maybe somebody out there is looking for a pet.
S: So what should someone do if they want one?
C: They should email me. My email is chrisdalaras@hotmail.com
S: Thank you Chris. He's got four lovely black and white kittens and he's not asking any money for them and his email is chrisdalaras@hotmail.com Over to you, Jules.

4

Juliet: Right! Our next caller is called...
Keith: Keith!
J: And what are you selling, Keith?
K: A mobile phone, it's a latest model Nokia and I only want € 100 for it. It's quite new.
J: Keith, why are you selling it?
K: Because my family are leaving the country.
J: Where are you going?
K: Oh, we're moving back to Scotland. I can't use it there.
J: Are you looking forward to living in Scotland?
K: Oh, not really, I like it here more.
J: Oh well, never mind, you can always come back here. So if someone is interested in the phone –
K: Could they please phone me, the number is 655 83 52 68, that's 655 83 52 68, and the name is Keith.
J: Well, thank you Keith, good luck with selling the phone, and good luck back in Scotland.

5

Sue: The next caller is Barbara. Hello Barbara!
Barbara: Hello.
S: And what are you trying to sell, Barbara?
B: An electric guitar and some studio recording equipment.
S: So you're not playing music or composing music any more?
B: They're things that don't belong to me. I'm selling them for someone else, and I'm making some space in my house.
S: I see.
B: I'm changing a lot of things about the way I live. I'm re-organising my life completely.
S: Really? Good for you! And what about the price?
B: The guitar and the home studio? € 750.
S: And can you give us a contact phone or email?
B: Sure. The email is barbara70@yahoo.com
S: Let's just check that – barbara70@yahoo.com and she's offering a home recording studio with an electric guitar. Thank you, Barbara, and good luck with all these changes.
B: Thank you.
S: So, remember, if you've got something to sell, give us a call the same time next week.

TRACK 01 / CD 2 ▸▸ LOVE AND MARRIAGE

LISTENING

1 Ouça a faixa e responda em seu caderno as perguntas que seguem.

1. What is her job? / 2. Where did she work before? / 3. Why do so many people now contract a wedding planner? / 4. What skills does she need? / 5. Why does she think so many marriages are not successful nowadays?

2 Volte a escutá-la e responda a estas outras perguntas.

1. What does a bride sometimes forget? / 2. How many weddings does Gemma organise a year? / 3. How do couples usually contact her? / 4. Why does she recommend hiring a wedding planner? / 5. What is the most important thing in a marriage?

3 Escute atentamente as frases abaixo e as repita imitando a entonação.

How did you get involved with this?
How do you organise your work?
What are the key things you do?
Why do so many people these days contract a wedding organiser?
What skills do you need to be a good wedding organiser?
What advice would you give a couple who are going to get married?
Why do you think so many people get divorced these days?

VOCABULARY

Get

Get é um verbo muito usual em inglês. Combina com todo tipo de palavras e tem muitos significados distintos. Sua forma de passado é invariável: é sempre **got**.

A) **Get** + noun or pronoun

Quando acompanhado de um nome ou de um pronome tem o sentido de "obter", "conseguir", "receber", "pegar", "ganhar", "dar" (acarretar) ...

I **got a letter** from Lou this morning.	*Recebi uma carta de Lou esta manhã.*
If I listen to heavy metal music I **get a headache**.	*Se escuto heavy metal me dá uma dor de cabeça.*

É possível usar com dois objetos:

Can I **get you a drink**?	*Posso lhe servir algo para beber?*

B) **Get** + adjective

Acompanhado de adjetivo, normalmente tem o sentido de "mudar" ou "alterar".

As you **get old**, your sense of time changes.	*À medida que você envelhece, sua percepção do tempo altera.*
This computer is **getting worse** and worse.	*Este computador está se tornando cada vez pior.*

C) **Get** + adverb or preposition

Diante de um advérbio (como **away**, **up**, **out**) ou de uma preposição (**in**, **off**, **on**) expressa algum tipo de movimento.

I **get up** at 7.30 every day.	*Todos os dias me levanto às 7h30.*
He came to see me about it, but I told him to **get out**.	*Veio me ver para falar dele, mas eu disse a ele para ir embora.*
Alex felt strange as he **got on** the plane.	*Alex começou a se sentir mal assim que subiu no avião.*

D) **Get** + -ing / **Get** + infinitive

Nestes casos expressa a ideia de uma mudança ou desenvolvimento gradativo.

Finding an inexpensive place to live is **getting** impossible in this town.	*Encontrar um lugar barato nesta cidade está ficando impossível.*
I **got to know** how the company works quite well.	*Acabei conhecendo muito bem o funcionamento da empresa.*

4 Nesta faixa são empregadas muitas combinações com **get**. Classifique os empregos a seguir em um dos usos anteriores: a, b, c ou d.

1. How did you **get involved** with this?
2. We **got tired** of having a boss.
3. We decided to **get out**.
4. The wedding can **get** quite **chaotic**.
5. A couple **get engaged** and then maybe do a search...
6. I **get a good idea** about the kind of wedding they want.
7. More people **are getting divorced** these days because...
8. If they come to us for a second wedding they **get a discount**!

Married to or married with?

Compare: **She's married to Mark / She's married with three children**.

GRAMMAR

Have (got) to + infinitive

Gemma diz **You have to be very organised** e **We have to provide all the services the couple need within the budget they have**. A construção **have/has got to** + infinitivo expressa a ideia de obrigação, como "ter que" em português. A forma no passado é **had to** (invariável).

A politician **has to make** a lot of difficult decisions.
We **had to change** our plans because of the bad weather.
Do you **have to work** Saturdays?

Take-away English

Do they go together?	Eles vão juntos/as?
I wouldn't say everything.	Eu não diria tudo.
Some do and some don't.	Alguns sim e outros não.

CULTURAL note

Many years ago, the idea of having a **boyfriend** or **girlfriend** didn't exist. Your parents arranged a marriage with someone who was considered right for you, and that is still true in many parts of the world. This is called an **arranged marriage**, in contrast to a marriage for love or a love marriage. Before you **get married**, normally you **get engaged** first. The person who you are going to marry is called your **fiancé** (a man) or **fiancée** (a woman), both words that come from French. On the day of the **wedding**, the fiancée is the **bride** and the fiancé is the **groom**, or **bridegroom**. After the wedding, the **best man**, usually a close friend of the groom's, **makes a speech** and asks all the guests to **toast** the happy couple, usually with champagne. Before the wedding, the best man is also responsible for the **wedding ring** (or rings), which symbolises the marriage. Normally, one or more unmarried or single sisters of the couple is/are **bridesmaids**. Instead of a traditional marriage, a lot of people nowadays prefer to live together, or have a civil union, and recently many countries have recognised **single sex union**, or gay marriage.

Glossary

arranged marriage: casamento arranjado	**fiancée**: noivo/noiva	sexo
best man: padrinho	**girlfriend**: namorada	**to make a speech**: fazer um discurso
boyfriend: namorado	**to get married**: casar-se	**to toast**: brindar
bride: noiva	**to get engaged**: noivar-se	cerimônia (casamento)
bridesmaid: dama de honra	**groom**: noivo	**wedding ring**: aliança (de casamento)
bridegroom: noivo	**single sex union**: união de pessoas do mesmo	
fiancé/		

Glossary

a bit	um pouco	couple	casal
at least	pelo menos	demanding	exigente
be able to (to)	poder, ser capaz de	discount	desconto
between	entre	dream	sonho
boss	chefe	event	evento
bouquet	buquê	florist	florista
bride	noiva	follow (to)	seguir
bring (to)	trazer, levar	forget (to)	esquecer
budget	orçamento	hairdresser	cabeleireiro
celebrant	aquele que celebra a missa	hire (to)	contratar
		key	chave
chaotic	caótico, confuso	kind	tipo

leave (to)	deixar, esquecer	search	busca, procura
long	grande	set up (to)	montar
make an effort (to)	esforçar-se	sort out (to)	solucionar
manicurist	manicure	split up (to)	separar-se, acabar um relacionamento
market	mercado		
marriage	casamento	spring	primavera
match (to)	combinar	strict	estrito, restrito
message	mensagem	successful (to be)	ser um sucesso
miracle	milagre	suggestion	sugestão
musician	músico	suitable	apropiado/a
on behalf of	em nome de	summer	verão
otherwise	se não	supplier	fornecedor/a
pay a visit (to)	retribuir uma visita	tip	conselho, dica
photographer	fotógrafo/a	venue	local de um evento
price	preço, valor	waste of money	perder dinheiro
provide (to)	oferecer	wedding	cerimônia
real time	tempo real	within	dentro de

Transcript

Brian: Right, love and marriage: do they go together? With me I have Gemma Sala, Gemma Sala, who knows all about it.

Gemma: Well, come on, I wouldn't say everything. I'm a wedding organiser.

B: What's your market, Gemma?

G: My market is English-speaking weddings.

B: And what does a wedding organiser do, Gemma? Do you help someone find a husband or a wife? Do you help people to get together?

G: Oh no, Brian, I'm afraid that's the only thing that we cannot provide. What a wedding organiser does is help a couple to organise their dream wedding, providing products and services they need for their event to be successful. A wedding organiser also co-ordinates the wedding on the day, making sure that everything is okay, and sorting out little problems that might appear in real time, for example the bride forgets to bring the bouquet, maybe she's left it in the hotel and then we send someone from our team to get it.

B: I see. And how did you – how did you get involved with this?

G: My business partner and I were working for a software company and we got tired of having a boss and helping him make money. We decided to get out, so we set up our own business and we thought weddings were a good thing because people always get married.

B: And how do you organise your work?

G: You have to be very organised because I personally organise at least twelve weddings a year, and each one is a lot of work. Brides are usually very demanding, which means you need to follow a strict calendar, otherwise the wedding can get quite chaotic.

B: Are these weddings all through

the year, or are they concentrated in spring and summer?

G: Usually they're concentrated between the months of May and September.

B: Okay, fine. And what are the key things you do?

G: Well, a couple get engaged and then maybe do a search for a wedding planner on the Internet. When they leave us a message asking about our services I get in touch with them and I ask them a lot of questions to be able to provide them with different options – maybe they need to find a suitable reception venue, I ask them some questions so this way I get a good idea about the kind of wedding they want and then I make some suggestions to match that. I get pictures for them, and information about prices and conditions. The same happens with other products and services like photographers, videographers, hairdressers, manicurists, florists, musicians, and celebrants etc.

B: Don't all couples want those things?

G: Some do and some don't. We also negotiate the price on behalf of the client, because apart from organising the event we are also budget managers. Because we have to provide all the services the couple need within the budget they have. And then finally we co-ordinate the event on the day.

B: Right, so why do so many people these days contract a wedding organiser?

G: Well, basically because these days people work so many hours and don't have time to spend hours looking for suppliers on the Internet, making enquiries, paying visits, negotiating prices etc.

B: And they get you to do all that?

G: Yes, basically.

B: What skills do you need to be a good wedding organiser?

G: Be patient, extremely organised, you need to have good negotiation skills, be very quick and resolute in difficult moments and of course have good communication skills.

B: And what advice would you give a couple who are going to get married?

G: Hire a wedding planner. Sometimes people don't do it because they think it's a waste of money they're often wrong, because wedding planners organise so many weddings a year which means we know the best suppliers for the best prices and can give you prices that you would never be able to get.

B: Why do you think so many people get divorced these days?

G: I think that more people are getting divorced these days because they haven't got the same patience that people used to have before, and when they have the first difficult moment they decide to split up or get separated instead of making all the effort necessary to make it work.

B: But if they get married again that's more business for you, isn't it?

G: I think if they come to us for a second wedding they get a discount!

B: So any tips for a long, loving, successful marriage?

G: I haven't got a miracle recipe but I think good communication with your partner is the best thing for a long and happy marriage.

B: Thanks very much, Gemma

G: You're welcome, Brian.

B: Now, what song would you like to hear?

G: *Love and marriage* by Frank Sinatra.

B: That was Gemma Sala. And here's the song.

TRACK 02 / CD 2 ▶▶   **FIRST LOVE**

LISTENING

1 Assinale a opção correta.

JULIET

1. was in love when she was a teenager with...
   - a) a teacher
   - b) another girl
   - c) a schoolmate
   - d) someone called Stephen

2. first met her husband...
   - a) at school
   - b) at work
   - c) at a job interview
   - d) at a rugby match

SUE

1. had her first romance...
   - a) with a very popular boy
   - b) with a teacher
   - c) with a timid boy
   - d) with a golfer

2. was very unhappy when the boy...
   - a) didn't go to the school dance
   - b) went with his *ex* to the dance
   - c) didn't want to dance
   - d) went to university

STUART

1. met his first girlfriend...
   - a) at a party
   - b) at university
   - c) when he was 15
   - d) in a chatroom

2. met his wife...
   - a) in Bali
   - b) at a party
   - c) at a language school
   - d) at university

2 Coloque **T** ou **F** de acordo com o que se viu. Reescreva as falsas.

JULIET...
- 1. first kissed a boy when she was 5 or 6.
- 2. had a lot of competitors for the boy that she liked when she was at school.
- 3. lived with her partner for three years before they got married.

SUE...
- 1. was at a school where there were four boys to every girl.
- 2. had to be careful with her school romance because her father was a teacher at the school.
- 3. and her first boyfriend continued to be friends after their separation.

STUART...
- 1. wasn't confident about girls when he was a teenager.
- 2. was with his first girlfriend at university.
- 3. got married in India.

VOCABULARY

3 Relacione os seguintes verbos e expressões com sua tradução.

1	to ask somebody out	a	partir o coração de alguém
2	to break up	b	apaixonar-se
3	to break somebody's heart	c	casar-se
4	to chat somebody up	d	convidar para sair
5	to fall in love	e	acabar (uma relação)
6	to get married	f	começar a viver juntos
7	to kiss	g	paquerar
8	to make eye contact	h	continuar juntos
9	to move in	i	estar juntos
10	to be together	j	beijar
11	to stay together	k	trocar olhares

4 Coloque esses verbos no passado e na coluna correta.

Regular verbs	Irregular verbs

5 Ordene, segundo seus próprios critérios, as diferentes fases de uma relação.

- he/she asked him/her out
- he/she chatted him/her up
- they fell in love
- they made eye contact
- they moved in together
- he/she broke his/her heart
- they broke up
- they got married
- they got engaged
- they kissed

6 O relacionamento anterior acabou mal. Tente descrever uma relação que acabe bem. Use o **simple past** para épocas já passadas.

7 Relacione outros verbos e expressões com sua tradução.

1	to be in love (with someone)	a	um beijo
2	a couple	b	parceiro/a
3	to have a crush (on someone)	c	um casal
4	an infatuation	d	estar apaixonado por alguém
5	a kiss	e	uma separação
6	a partner	f	ter uma queda por alguém
7	a separation	g	o amor de sua vida
8	the love of your life	h	loucura, obsessão

8 Complete as frases abaixo com as palavras e expressões das atividades 3 e 7.

1. Well, I've met lots of nice women, but I don't think I've met .... yet. Maybe this year.

2. If you're trying to .... , please stop now. I'm happily married.

3. You should be more proactive; if you like him, why don't you .... ?

4. Oh, is this man Julio your friend or is he your .... ?

5. If you're not really happy, you have to .... with her. It's as simple as that.

6. You know, I .... with you the moment I first saw you, getting off the train.

7. My parents don't like the idea of you and me living together before we ....

8. • Where do .... first meet?
   • Many at university, and a lot at work, not so many in pubs.

9. It took me three years to feel okay again about relationships after she ....

10. When she looks at me like that I know she wants me to .... her.

GRAMMAR

Past continuous

Juliet utiliza o **past continuous** para descrever as circunstâncias que rodeiam um acontecimento concreto do passado. O acontecimento principal conjuga-se no **simple past**.

I **was living** in London, and **looking** for a job, and this man interviewed me for a job, and of course I got it...

A forma é sempre esta:

> sujeito + **was** ou **were** + verbo em **-ing**

9 Todas as frases abaixo foram retiradas da gravação. Volte a escutá-la prestando atenção na pronúncia de **was/were**. Em seguida, repita em voz alta.

I **was** living in London, and looking for a job...
I **was** always falling in love.
I **was** studying at a school with 700 boys and only 25 girls.
My father **was** teaching there.
I **was** dying to find a girlfriend.
Suddenly I **was** chatting up this beautiful, brilliant, girl.
We **were** both studying at a language school.
We **were** living in Indonesia.

Shall I / Shall we

Juliet diz: **Shall I go first?** ("Eu começo primeiro?"). **Shall I** ou **Shall we** é uma construção muito habitual para sugerir ou oferecer. A forma é a seguinte:

> **shall I** ou **shall we** + infinitivo sem **to**

- **Shall we** have a break for coffee?   *Vamos fazer uma pausa para um*
- Yes, why not?   *café? / Sim. E por que não?*
- **Shall I** help you with that?   *Quer que te ajude com isso?*
- No thanks, I'm okay.   *Não, obrigado, não precisa.*

Had to

Como já vimos, **had to** é o passado de **have to**. A construção é:

> sujeito + **had to** + infinitivo

I **had to** be very careful.   We decided we **had to** get married.

Take-away English

Nesta faixa são utilizadas muitas frases curtas, como **Go on!** ("Continue!"), **Well done!** ("Muito bem!"), **How awful!** ("Péssimo!"). A construção How + adjetivo é muito comum em frases como: **How cool** ("Que legal!"), **How exciting** ("Que divertido!"), **How sad** ("Que triste") etc. Atenção! **How come?** é uma pergunta que significa "por quê?" (como Why?).

Para referir-se à vez (turno, hora), são empregadas as expressões **Your turn** ("Sua vez"), **My turn** ("Minha vez"), **Jim's turn** ("É a vez do Jim") etc.

I ended up doing something expressa o resultado de algo ("Acabei fazendo algo"). Outro exemplo: **I don't know how I ended up living here** ("Não sei como acabei morando aqui").

Right from the start significa "desde o começo". Um exemplo: **We've been in this project right from the start** ("Estamos neste projeto desde o começo").

I never stood a chance significa "Eu nunca tive oportunidade". É possível substituir **never** pelo verbo **do**, embora isso implique uma mudança no verbo principal. Por exemplo: **The independent candidate for the Presidency of the USA didn't stand a chance** ("O candidato independente à presidência dos Estados Unidos não teve chance alguma").

CULTURAL note

Education in the UK

Education is compulsory in Britain from the age of 5 to 16. Most children go to **state schools**, called *maintained schools* because the government maintains them. There are also faith or religious schools where children who are Roman Catholic, Jewish or Muslim etc receive instruction in their religion. About 17% of children go to faith schools. About 5% of children go to private secondary schools, which are called *public schools*. Why are they called *public schools* if they are private? Because when they were founded, they were open to the sons of the public in general. They were originally free, but later started to charge **fees** and they became schools for a rich élite. Public schools are now called *independent schools*, and most of them are **boarding schools**, like the one Harry Potter goes to. Children attend primary school until they are 10-11. In most parts of Britain there is no academic selection to enter secondary schools. At the age of 16, children do GCSE (General Certificate of Secondary Education) exams, and two years later, at the same school or at a sixth-form college, they do GCE **A levels**, usually no more than four **subjects**, and usually these are the subjects that the students plan to study later at university. Some secondary schools, like Sue's, have pupils who are given special responsibility to monitor and discipline their **schoolmates**, like a kind of school police, and they are called *prefects*.

Education in the USA

Generally speaking, education is compulsory in the USA from the age of 6 to 16, but every state makes its own regulations, and most children stay at school to the age of 18. From the age of 6 to 12, children go to Elementary School, and then go on to a Junior High School, from 12-13 and finally High School, from 14-18.

The four years of High School have names: *Freshman*, *Sophomore*, *Junior* and *Senior*. At the end of High School, the university entrance **qualification** is called the High School Diploma, which is **awarded** in a formal graduation ceremony. High Schools make and sell a book every year with the photo **portraits** of all the students and all the teachers, and this is called a **yearbook**. It's normal for the yearbook to have a section with photos of the most attractive students, the students who will most probably succeed professionally, and everybody writes dedicatory comments about their classmates. American High Schools appear often in films and TV programmes, frequently **highlighting** the sporting aspects and social ones, especially the elegant gala ball (or dance) at the end of the course, called *the Senior Prom*.

Glossary

A level: qualificação acadêmica	**fee:** cota, taxa	**to award:** outorgar, aprovar
boarding school: internato	**portrait:** foto	**to highlight:** ressaltar, destacar
	qualification: qualificação conferida aos estudantes	
	state school: escola pública	
	subject: disciplina	**yearbook:** anuário

Glossary

afterwards	depois, mais tarde
agony	agonia
ask out (to)	convidar para sair
awful	terrível, horrível
boarding school	internato
boy	menino
briefly	por pouco tempo
call back (to)	retornar um telefonema
captain	capitão
choose (to)	escolher
clothes	roupa
couple (a)	casal
current	atual
cynicism	cinismo
die (to)	morrer
disbelief	incredulidade
each other	cada um/a
embarrassed	envergonhado/a
end (to)	terminar, acabar
foreigner	estrangeiro/a
friend	amigo/a
golf course	campo de golfe
graduate (to)	graduar-se
hard	difícil, complicado/a
how come?	por quê?
high society	alta sociedade
in the long run	a longo prazo
infamous	infame, desprezível
interview (to)	entrevistar

joke	brincadeira, piada	school prefect	monitor (escola particular)
laugh (to)	rir	sign	letreiro (placa)
learn (to)	aprender	somehow	de alguma maneira
lesson	lição	sort of	até certo ponto
meet (to)	conhecer	stand a chance (to)	ter uma oportunidade
messy	complicado/a, confuso/a	suddenly	de repente
mouth	boca	suppose (to)	supor
novel	romance (livro)	take sides (to)	tomar partido
papers	papéis (documentação de estrangeiros)	teach (to)	ensinar
		teenager	adolescente
physical	físico	tongue	língua
real life	vida real	tree	árvore
sadness	tristeza	tremendous	genial
school ball	baile da escola	unsuitable	inapropriado/a

Transcript

Stuart: Okay, now we've heard from the expert in weddings, but what about you? You know, in novels the story often ends with the marriage but in real life the marriage often ends the story. So what about you? What was your first experience of love? What happened? How did you meet the love of your life?

Sue: Wow – that's a hard question

Juliet: Is it? Shall I go first then?

S: Yeah – go on Jules!

J: I remember the first time I kissed a boy. I was five or six, and Stephen was my special friend so I kissed him!

S: Hooray!

J: Then as a teenager I had one of those awful crushes that everyone laughs about, but they are agony at the time. Of course he was the captain of the school rugby team, and all the other girls were in love with him as well, so I never stood a chance.

St: Too bad!

S: Oh god, not that. Go on, go on...

J: As a young woman I was always falling in love but only briefly and usually with unsuitable men, so I suppose that was more infatuation really. I think the first time I really fell in love was when I was 23. I was living in London, and looking for a job, and this man interviewed me for a job, and of course I got it, and he asked me out the next day, so we went out the next day and the next, and as the song says "It was just one of those things".

St: Yeah, yeah, and?

J: And we moved in together a month later and got married two years after that.

S: That was easy!

J: Well, sort of easy.

St: Sue, what about you?

S: I was studying at a school with 700 boys and only 25 girls.

J: Hooray!

S: He was a school prefect and in the school rugby team, and he was very popular and respected.

J: This sounds like my story!

S: We started walking home regularly together and making eye contact. I lived at the school.

J: How come?
S: Because my father was teaching there and it was a boarding school. So I had to be very careful. Very careful. So, we met after school, we went to a golf course that was next to the school – yes, a golf course, no bad jokes, please! Our physical romantic adventures consisted of passionate kissing in the trees at the golf course, and then we went home; me to my home and him to his.
St: And what happened?
S: Tragedy! The school ball.
J: Oh, the high school dance.
S: No, more than a dance, this was a ball, formal clothes, waltzes and foxtrots, high society. He decided to invite his ex-girlfriend to the infamous ball.
St: No!
S: And I was left without a partner.
J: How awful!
St: Did you talk to him again?
S: I think he was highly embarrassed, and he found it very difficult to ever speak to me again. As for me, for months I was in complete shock and disbelief, and absolutely destroyed with sadness. Everyone knew that we were a couple, all our friends, and this obvious separation gave people a great opportunity to talk, some to take sides and I suppose in the long run, it was a lesson to learn from. Yes, I had to learn from that experience.
St: And afterwards?
S: He graduated from the school and went to university. I continued at the school, and I still had 699 boys to choose from. And since then I have always maintained a certain cynicism about love, but then I did manage to break my heart again on two future occasions in my life, but that's far too messy to discuss!

J: Great! Come on, Stuart, your turn!
St: Well, when I was 16, like a lot of other sixteen year old boys, I was dying to find a girlfriend, but I didn't really know how to start. Then one night I found myself at a friend's party, sitting on the sofa, and suddenly I was chatting up this beautiful, brilliant, girl, and somehow, we just ended up with our tongues in each other's mouths. Her name was Elizabeth, and we were together for a couple of years until we went to different universities, and we decided to break up.
S: But that was a good start, Stuart. Well done!
J: And how did you meet your current partner?
St: We were both studying at a language school. She, Bel, put up a sign at the language school asking for someone who wanted to do an English-Spanish language exchange. A couple of people called, but I was the one who knew the least Spanish, so she called me back. I liked her right from the start, but it didn't get romantic for at least a month. We've been living together for 17 years now.
J: For 17 years – that's tremendous.
S: Excuse me, you are married, aren't you?
St: Oh yes. Okay, we were living in Indonesia.
S: Indonesia!
St: Yeah, Indonesia, but Bel couldn't get papers because we weren't married, so we decided we had to get married, and we got married in Bali because that was the only place where they would marry a couple of foreigners.
J: How romantic getting married in Bali!
S: I think staying together for 17 years is more romantic, myself.

TRACK 03 / CD 2 ▶▶ TEENAGERS & PARENTS

LISTENING

1 Ouça a faixa e complete o quadro.

Who / Whose	Lewis	Liam	both
1. Whose mother asks questions about who he goes out with?			
2. Whose mother doesn't like him to stay much in the house?			
3. Whose mother gives him a time limit for video games?			
4. Whose mother thinks his video games are too violent?			
5. Who says it's important to remember that violent games are not real?			
6. Who has problems with his brother when they play *Playstation*?			
7. Who says he has few problems with watching the TV programmes he likes?			
8. Who says he has a good relationship with his parents?			

2 True (T) or false (F)? Assinale e reescreva as falsas.

1. Lewis's father asks him more questions than his mother.
2. Liam's mum always wants to know which friends he has been with.
3. Lewis feels that his parents are more generous with his older brother.
4. Liam's Mum likes to know what TV programmes he watches after 9 pm.
5. Lewis's couldn't go the concert because his parents didn't know his friend.

....

....

....

VOCABULARY

Phrasal verbs

Já vimos alguns **phrasal verbs**, como **break up** ("acabar uma relação"), **chat up** ("cantar alguém"), **end up (doing something)** ("acabar fazendo algo"), entre outros.

3 Veja agora outros **phrasal verbs**; todos retirados da faixa. Leia a transcrição e dê o significado de cada um.

> go out · stay out · get on with · end up · pick up · make up

fazer as pazes: .... sair: ....
pegar (buscar) alguém: .... acabar fazendo alguma coisa: ....
dar-se bem: .... ficar de fora: ....

4 Indique se as frases a seguir estão corretas ou incorretas. Veja se você consegue corrigir as incorretas. Faça isso em seu caderno.

	correct	incorrect
1. I have to **pick up** Mrs Clover at the airport at 10.15.		
2. Would you like to **go** tonight?		
3. Do you **get on well** your parents **with**?		
4. My parents let me **stay out** until 2 a.m.		
5. We **ended** us **up** living with her parents for a year.		
6. We had a few problems in summer, but we've **made up** since then.		

5 Agora, responda a estas perguntas em seu caderno.

When you were a teenager...
- did you **get on** with your parents?
- did you **get on** with your brother(s) and sister(s)?
- did you **go out** very much on Fridays, Saturdays and Sundays?
- what time did you **stay out** until?

GRAMMAR

Adverbs of frequency

6 Escute o fragmento abaixo e preencha as lacunas com advérbios de frequência.

Lewis: Well my mother especially is very inquisitive about who I go out with, and she .... sets a time, although my dad is .... more understanding about why I'd like to stay out longer with my friends.
Brian: What about you, Liam?
Lewis: Mum .... lets me go without too many problems. In fact, she .... prefers me to go out instead of being stuck in the house all day. But she .... gives me a time to be back and she .... asks me where I've been and who I've been with.

7 Na faixa aparecem os advérbios **generally**, **hardly ever**, **quite often**, **always** e **usually**. Ordene-os. Há dois que vão na mesma coluna.

Less often				More often
never				

Releia o fragmento anterior. Onde vão normalmente estes advérbios na frase?

Let

Liam e Lewis dizem: **Mum usually lets me go without too many problems.**/ **... but they still let me go out**. O verbo **let** é empregado para expressar consentimento. Equivale ao verbo português "deixar". A estrutura é sempre a seguinte:

> **let** + somebody + infinitive (without **to**)

Let é um verbo irregular. Sua forma de passado é **let**.

Let me help you with that.	*Deixe-me ajudá-lo nisso.*
Our teacher **let** us go ten minutes early today.	*Nosso professor nos deixou sair hoje 10 minutos mais cedo.*

Take-away English

Liam diz: **Yeah, I get on pretty well with my mum.** É muito comum pronunciar yes como **yeah** na língua oral.

Quando Lewis diz **My parents are fine with me watching TV** quer dizer que seus pais não se incomodam que ele veja TV. A forma básica da expressão é **I'm fine with that**, que significa algo como "Por mim, nenhum problema". Note que, se há um verbo depois, ele deve ser conjugado no gerúndio (**-ing**).

Liam diz: **Mum usually lets me go without too many problems.** A construção **too + adjective** ("demasiadamente") indica algum tipo de inconveniente: **too expensive** ("caro demais"), **too far** ("longe demais"), **too little** ("pouco demais"), **too late** ("tarde demais"). Atenção! A expressão **Too bad!** significa "Que azar!", normalmente em tom de ironia.

Glossary

adult theme	temática para adultos	mum	mamãe
afterwards	depois	often	frequentemente
although	ainda que	on his own	só, sozinho
argue (to)	discutir	permission	permissão
basically	basicamente	pick someone up (to)	pegar (buscar) alguém
dad	papai		
favour (to)	ser parcial, favorecer	pretty	bastante
fight (to)	brigar, lutar	afterwards	depois
for real	de verdade	quite	completamente
frustrating	frustrante	set a time (to)	marcar um horário
get on with (to)	dar-se bem com alguém	smaller	menor
		stuff	coisas (informal)
go out (to)	sair	stuck (in the house)	preso em casa
game	jogo		
hardly ever	quase nunca	thankful	agradecido/a
in fact	de fato	too + adjective	demasiado/a
inquisitive	questionador/a	understanding	compreensivo/a
longer	mais tempo	violent	violento/a
lucky	sortudo/a	whether	se (condicional)
make up (to)	fazer as pazes		

Transcript

Brian: So today I'm with Liam and Lewis and we're talking about whether teenagers – whether teenagers and parents can ever understand each other. You know – what about going out and staying out?

Lewis: Well my mother especially is very inquisitive about who I go out with, and she usually sets a time, although my dad is usually more understanding about why I'd like to stay out longer with my friends.

B: What about you, Liam?

Liam: Mum usually lets me go without too many problems. In fact, she usually prefers me to go out instead of being stuck in the house all day. But she always gives me a time to be back and she always asks me where I've been and who I've been with.

B: And what about things you play with – you know – games at home and stuff?

L: Well I enjoy playing my video console, so my mum puts a time limit on that and she doesn't like the type of games that I play.

B: Why not?

L: She says they're too violent.

B: Too violent? What do you think?

L: I don't think they're so bad.

B: Lewis?

Lw: Yes, it's basically the same problems as Liam, but I think that with violent games if you understand that they're not for real then there's no problem.

B: Okay and what about – you know – your brother, and how you get on with your brother?

Lw: Well, when we play *Playstation* together, which is quite often, we usually end up fighting for all kinds of different reasons and well, then my parents usually favour my brother because he's the smaller one. And then he can usually play on his own afterwards without asking their permission.

B: That must be very frustrating for you.

Lw: Yes, very.

B: Ok. What about the TV programmes that you watch? Any restrictions?

L: If it's after 9 o'clock my mum asks what I'm watching, but we usually watch TV together so it's hardly ever a problem.

Lw: My parents are fine with me watching TV except when it's – when the programmes have an adult theme or – the programmes are just very stupid.

B: In general, would you say that you have a good relationship with your parents?

Lw: Yes, well, I think generally they understand me quite well.

B: Right. Can you think of an example when they understood you recently?

Lw: Er – Yes. Well last week I wanted to go to a concert with my friends, and the friends came to pick me up pretty late, but they still let me. And they didn't know the boy I was going out with very well, but they still let me go out, and I was quite thankful for that.

B: Liam, what about you?

L: Yeah, I get on pretty well with my mum, we get on pretty well. We argue quite often, but then we just make up.

B: Okay, thanks, thanks very much.

TRACK 04 / CD 2 ▶▶   **PETER LOVEDAY**

LISTENING

1 Coloque **T** ou **F** em cada opção, corrigindo as incorretas.

1. Peter's present group…
   - a) has four instruments
   - b) is acoustic
   - c) started playing 5 years ago

2. Peter started playing music…
   - a) at university
   - b) in the 1980s
   - c) in London

3. Peter started singing…
   - a) at school
   - b) in church
   - c) in Australia

4. Peter also works…
   - a) in publishing
   - b) in teaching
   - c) in education

2 Ordene (1, 2, 3) os acontecimentos importantes na vida de Peter Loveday.

- He moved to London.
- He started playing with his present group.
- He started writing his own songs.

3 Agora, responda às perguntas abaixo.

1. Which types of music does he like? ....
2. How many songs will his next record have? ....

VOCABULARY

Fun or funny?

Tanto **fun** quanto **funny** podem ser traduzidos como "divertido", mas não são empregados exatamente da mesma forma. Usamos **fun** para expressar a ideia de "curtir", "desfrutar".

Come to the party; it'll be **fun**.   *Venha à festa; será divertido.*
We had a lot of **fun** last night.   *Curtimos muito ontem à noite.*

Usamos **funny** para nos referir a algo que nos alegra.

You said that the film was **funny**, but it didn't make us laugh.
And *now* the government wants to change its policies? That's *really* **funny**!

Funny, em alguns casos, equivale a "estranho", "esquisito".

Your friend is a bit **funny**, isn't he?   *Seu amigo é um pouco esquisito, não?*
This lasagne tastes **funny**.   *Esta lasanha tem um gosto estranho.*

4 Sublinhe (**underline**) a palavra correta e risque (**cross out**) a incorreta.

1. "What did you think of the new Woody Allen film?" "We liked it, but it wasn't as **fun** / **funny** as some of his other films."
2. We don't have to go out tonight; we can stay home and have just as much **fun** / **funny**.
3. I didn't like the Philosophy exam at all. They asked us some really **fun** / **funny** questions.
4. He thinks he's so **fun** / **funny**, but he doesn't amuse me at all.
5. We were in a traffic jam for six hours. It was no **fun** / **funny**, I can tell you.
6. Are you looking for a serious relationship, or do you just want to have **fun** / **funny**?
7. Your birthday is May 29th? That's **fun** / **funny** - mine is the same day!
8. Maybe it was because of the champagne, but everything he said seemed so **fun** / **funny**.
9. I didn't want to laugh, but she looked so **fun** / **funny** with tomato sauce all over her wedding dress.
10. Walking up a mountain at night to have a picnic? That sounds like **fun** / **funny**. I'll come.

Play

O verbo **play** normalmente é traduzido como "jogar".

Have you ever **played** golf?   *Você já jogou golfe alguma vez?*
Nadal **played** brilliantly in the final.   *Nadal jogou muito bem na final.*

Também é empregado para instrumentos musicais, com o sentido de "tocar".

You've always wanted to **play** the piano, now's your chance!

Também se usa com CD ou DVD no sentido de "pôr para tocar".

You're always **playing** the same CD. **Play** something else for a change!

Também se usa com o sentido de "interpretar" antes do nome de um personagem de uma obra de teatro ou de um filme.

Who did your prefer – Kenneth Branagh or Mel Gibson **playing** *Hamlet*?

A pessoa que joga é o "jogador", em inglês **player**.

Three **players** – two Greek and one French – received red cards in the match.

Como em português, **play** ("brincar") é o que fazem as crianças.

Stop **playing** now; it's time for bed.

De **play** se forma o adjetivo **playful** ("brincalhão", "divertido").

You're quite **playful** tonight; what's going on?

O substantivo **play** ("jogo", "jogada") é incontável.

Children learn a lot through **play**.

Play também significa "peça de teatro".

My favourite **play** is *Romeo and Juliet*.

Há muitas expressões com **play**, como **play a vital/key role** ("desempenhar um papel importante"), **play the fool** ("fazer papel de bobo"), **play a joke/trick on someone** ("tirar um sarro de alguém"), **a play on words** ("jogo de palavras") etc., e verbos como **play down** ("subestimar", "menosprezar").

Get on (with)

Peter diz: **This is what I like about this band, we get on very well and we work well together.** To get on (with someone) significa "dar-se bem com alguém".

My sister and I only started to **get on** well when we became adults.
I'm not saying it's his fault – we just don't **get on**.

Get on with something significa "dar continuidade".

I know this technology isn't ideal, but we just have to **get on with** the job.
My separation wasn't easy, but you have to **get on with** life, don't you?

GRAMMAR

Past simple vs. Present Perfect

5 Escute a gravação e complete o diálogo.

- So how many albums ▬▬▬▬ ▬▬▬▬ ▬▬▬▬?
- ▬▬▬▬ ▬▬▬▬ five, so far, but –
- Go on, tell us. What are you working on at the moment?
- I'm working on new songs for an album that we're going to record next year. ▬▬▬▬ ▬▬▬▬ seven songs for it.

Neste fragmento, Peter usa o **present perfect**, que já vimos na faixa 8. Ele é construído com **have/has** + particípio. É empregado quando nos referimos a algo que tenhamos feito até o momento, podendo continuar fazendo. Compare:

Elvis Presley **made** a lot of records.   *Elvis Presley gravou muitos discos.*
Shakira **has made** a lot of records.   *Shakira gravou (tem gravado) muitos discos.*

Também empregamos o **present perfect** para coisas que situamos em um tempo que tem relação com o presente (esta manhã, hoje, este mês, este ano...). Se o marco temporal já chegou ao fim, usamos o **simple past**. Compare estas duas frases:

We'**ve talked** about this question three times **this week**.
We **talked** about this question three times **last week**.

Irregular past participles

6 A maioria dos particípios são regulares, mas não todos. Complete o quadro da página seguinte com estes particípios irregulares:

> had · written · taken · begun · eaten · given · spoken · driven · seen
> drunk · known · come · made

infinitive	past	past participle
be	was/were	**been**
begin	began	
come	came	
drink	drank	
drive	drove	
eat	ate	
give	gave	
have	had	
know	knew	
make	made	
see	saw	
speak	spoke	
take	took	
write	wrote	

7 Sublinhe a opção correta em cada caso.

1. Don't tell me now that you don't want to go to the Springsteen concert! **I've bought** / **I bought** the tickets.
2. On my way home last night **I saw** / **I've seen** something strange.
3. **Have you ever tried** / **Did you ever try** wine from Australia? No, we **haven't** / **didn't**.
4. Almodóvar **has made** / **made** a lot of very successful, very famous films.
5. Italy **have won** / **won** the 2006 football World Cup.
6. When you were in Paris, **have you gone** / **did you go** to the Louvre?
7. I don't want to see that film again – **I've seen** / **I saw** it three times already.
8. Last year our salary costs **have gone up** / **went up** by 4%.
9. Can you help me? Yes, it's important – Jan **has lost** / **lost** his house keys.
10. Bob went to Athens for the first time in April but he **hasn't visited** / **didn't visit** the Acropolis!

Present Perfect Continuous

8 Complete este fragmento da faixa.

- How long _____ you _____ ?
- Singing? I suppose _____ since I was a boy.

A forma que se utiliza neste fragmento é o **present perfect continuous**, que é composto da seguinte maneira:

> **have/has** + **been** + the **-ing** form of the verb

Utilizamos este tempo para nos referir a algo que começou no passado, que tenha durado até agora e que talvez possa seguir por mais tempo. Costuma-se empregá-lo com **for** ("durante"), **since** ("desde") e **how long** ("quanto tempo").

I've been working here **for** 10 years.	*Há dez anos estou trabalhando aqui.*
We've been living in this house **since** 1997.	*Moramos nesta casa desde 1997.*
How long has he been playing for Inter Milan?	*Quanto tempo faz que ele joga na Inter de Milão?*

Atenção! Com verbos que não expressam uma ação, e sim um estado, empregamos o **present perfect** com as partículas **for**, **since** ou **how long**.

For many years **we've wanted** to move out of the city.	*Durante muitos anos quisemos morar fora da cidade.*
I've had this car **since** 2003.	*Tenho este carro desde 2003.*
How long have you been married for?	*Quanto tempo faz que você está casado?*

Usamos o **present perfect continuous** para algo que tem um resultado visível no momento atual, sem especificar quando começou a atividade.

What's wrong? **Have you been crying?**	*O que aconteceu? Você estava chorando?*
Slow down - **you've been working** too hard.	*Relaxe. Você tem trabalhado muito.*

9 Complete as frases abaixo com as seguintes formas no **present perfect continuous**.

> been looking for · been living · been going · been trying · been studying
> been watching · been growing · been playing · been driving · been learning

1. Have you really only _____ in this house for three months?
2. I've _____ Economics for two years, but I'd like to change to Psychology.
3. Since his divorce three years ago he's _____ a new woman in his life.
4. I imagine you're tired. You've _____ for eight hours.
5. Finally! Dani, do you know that I've _____ to phone you all day!
6. They've _____ really well recently, and they're now second in the league table.
7. Since she lost her job she's _____ to the gym every day for two hours.
8. How long have you _____ English?
9. Unemployment has _____ in this country since 2007.
10. I'm worried about Sam. He's _____ a lot of violent videos for the last few months.

10 Escute estes fragmentos da faixa prestando atenção principalmente em como se pronunciam os verbos auxiliares **have/has**. Identifique as palavras ou as sílabas que se pronunciam com mais ênfase e em seguida pronuncie estes fragmentos imitando sua pronúncia.

Well, for the past four years I've worked with the same musicians.
How long have you been singing?
I suppose I've been singing since I was a boy.
I like just about everything, but I've never really liked instrumental jazz.
So how many albums have you made?
I've written seven songs for it.

Take-away English

apart from that	fora isso
Glad you could join us!	Que bom que você está conosco!
* the late 70s	fim dos anos 1970
There are four of us.	Somos quarto.
What kind of...?	Que tipo de...?

* Da mesma maneira, é possível dizer **the early 90s** ("início dos anos 1990"), **the mid 60s** ("meados dos anos 1960") etc.

Glossary

above all	sobretudo	nice	legal, agradável
album	disco	none of us	nenhum de nós
arrangements	arranjos	organ	órgão
at a time	de uma vez	performance	atuação
at first	a princípio	produce (to)	produzir, fazer
band	grupo (de música)	public (in)	em público
buzz (to be a)	ser divertido	publisher	editor
choir	coro (de igreja)	quartet	quarteto
church	igreja	quite	bastante
cover version	versão (de uma música)	ready to go	pronto/a, acabado/a
danger	perigo, risco	record (to)	gravar
each	cada	sing (to)	cantar
enjoyable	agradável	singer-songwriter	cantor/a e compositor/a
favourite	preferido/a	song	canção, música
flute	flauta	sound	som
fun	divertido	stories	histórias
get on (to)	dar-se bem	strong	forte
get started (to)	começar	such a	tão, tanto/a
glad	contente	suppose (to)	supor
guitar	violão	those	aqueles/as
happen (to)	ocorrer, passar	together	juntos/as
harmony	harmonia	too	também
join (to)	unir-se, acompanhar	try (to)	experimentar
just about	quase quase	unique	único/a
kind	tipo, estilo	voice	voz
live	ao vivo	words	palavras
melody	melodia	work-wise	referente a trabalho
move (to)	mudar-se	write (to)	escrever, compor
my own	meu/s próprio/s		

Transcript

Peter: Hello my name's Peter Loveday and I'm a singer-songwriter.
Brian: Hello Peter. Glad you could join us today.
P: My pleasure.
B: Could you tell us about your work as a singer and song writer?
P: Well, for the past four years I've worked with the same musicians. We've performed in public a lot of times. There are four of us. We're a quartet: guitars, violin, percussion and sometimes a flute.
B: So it's acoustic music?
P: Basically yes, the music is quite acoustic and dynamic. It's a nice

sound. I like it. I write all the songs, but we work on the arrangements together. I love working with other people in this way. This is what I like about this band, we get on very well and we work well together.

B: Right, and how did you get started?

P: I started when I was at university, in Australia. At that time (the late 70s) a lot of interesting things were happening in popular music. People were trying new things. It was very DIY, Do-it-yourself. Everybody was in a band. It was fun. I started in a band that played cover versions of songs. At first none of us really knew how to play our instruments, and that made the band sound very "interesting". Later, I started writing my own songs, and very soon I only played my songs. Then the band moved to London and we lived there for about seven years. We were very poor but we recorded, and played quite a lot and generally we enjoyed living in London.

B: How long have you been singing?

P: Singing? I suppose I've been singing since I was a boy. When I was a boy I was in a church choir. It was such a buzz, so good – the sound of the organ, the voices and harmonies, those strong melodies.

B: Hmm. What kind of music do you like?

P: I like just about everything, but I've never really liked instrumental jazz. I like words and stories to go with the music, so I like pop music, country, blues, flamenco, classical music.

B: What about recording and live performances?

P: Above all, I love performing – usually – I think each performance is unique. I like the danger that's involved with performing live. I love performing too because I can express myself in a way that I normally can't do.

B: And recording?

P: Recording is interesting too. The last CD we made was recorded live, with everybody playing together. Usually people record one instrument at a time. Recording live is more dynamic and enjoyable.

B: So how many albums have you made?

P: I've made five, so far, but –

B: Go on, tell us. What are you working on at the moment?

P: I'm working on new songs for an album that we're going to record next year. I've written seven songs for it, and those songs are ready to go, but I still need to write five or six more.

B: Interesting. And apart from that, what do you do, work-wise?

P: I work for an educational publisher. We produce online courses and also books.

B: And what do you do to relax?

P: My favourite things to do are reading, watching movies, being with friends, and playing in my band.

B: Thank you very much; that was Peter Loveday, who's now going to give us a song.

P: Thank you, Brian.

Here I Am (Words and music by Peter Loveday)

Standing on the corner with a suitcase in my hand.
Never thought I'd leave this town, but here I am.
Life is full of crossroads, of corners to be turned,
ladders to climb, bridges to be burned.

Wind-made waves in a sea of maize, a cobalt field of sky.
Confined to the quarters of my heart, with an arrow in my eye.
Drive out there to where she lives, turn off the road blind,
to see her standing at the door, one last time.

I am reaping, reaping the crops I have sown.
I am leaving, leaving the land I have known.

There is nothing to me now, but the vacuum that I hide.
As we sit by the willow tree, she says goodbye.
Headlights caress the road ahead, the steering wheel held tight.
The vision of her standing there, in silence and in sunlight.

Stretching out across the land, there is no need to look.
That's the state I'm living in, the title of the book.
I know one day the lines will fade, I know it won't be soon.
Until that time she lingers on, the hounds are baying at the moon.

I am reaping, reaping in the crops I have sown.
I am leaving, leaving the land that I have known

Peter Loveday: Guitar/Vocals
Andy Gemmel: Guitar/Slide guitar
Andy Henley: Bass/Vocals

TRACK 05 / CD 2 ▶▶   FASHION

LISTENING

1 Ouça os primeiros 50 segundos da faixa e marque a opção correta.

1. The clothes collection that Sue is talking about:
   a) is a collection for next **spring-summer** / **autumn-winter**
   b) is a collection for **men** / **women** / **both**

Agora, escute o restante e marque as informações adequadas.

2. The collection:
   a) will have colours that are **brighter** / **less bright** than usual
   b) will have an **African** / **Asian** look
   c) will have **strong** / **subtle** designs
   d) will be about **25%** / **33%** / **50%** wool
   e) **will be** / **will not be** inexpensive

2 True or false? Indique e corrija as falsas.

	true	false
1. Sue thinks Stuart isn't influenced by fashion.		
2. Sue's definition of "young" is 18-25.		
3. Sleeves will be long and short depending on the climate.		
4. Cotton won't be used much.		
5. Prices for clothes will be in the 25-35 euro range.		

3 Complete o quadro.

Who...	Juliet	Sue	Stuart
1. is very tired			
2. will be busy with other people			
3. will be busy at home			
4. will have friends visiting			
5. doesn't like friends visiting			

VOCABULARY

Colours

4 Escreva a palavra em inglês ao lado de sua equivalente em português.

> black · blue · brown · green · grey · pink · purple · red · white · yellow

amarelo .... roxo ....
azul .... preto ....
branco .... vermelho ....
cinza .... rosa ....
marrom .... verde ....

Clothes

5 Escreva a palavra em inglês ao lado de sua equivalente em português.

> blouse · boots · bra · dress · jersey · leggings · socks · panties · shoes
> skirt · shirt · T-shirt · trousers · underpants

botas .... blusa ....
calça .... camisa ....
sutiã .... meias ....
camiseta .... calcinha ....
saia .... vestido ....
suéter .... cueca ....
sapatos .... calça legging ....

Materials

What are clothes made of? Sue fala de **cotton** ("algodão"), **wool** ("lã") e **synthetic fabrics** ("tecidos sintéticos"). Outros materias: **silk** ("seda") e **leather** ("couro", "pele").

6 Complete especificando a cor e os materiais das peças de roupa.

What are you wearing now?
I'm wearing ▮

One other person I know:
▮ is wearing ▮

Yesterday I was wearing: ▮

Two other people I know:
▮ was wearing ▮
▮ was wearing ▮

Fashion or what?

Em português, usa-se a palavra **fashion** como adjetivo ("Isso é *fashion*"), ainda que, de fato, ao menos em inglês, seja um substantivo que, combinando com outros substantivos, forma conceitos como **fashion show** ou **fashion industry**, mas o adjetivo é **fashionable** ("na moda"). Por exemplo: **a fashionable design, a fashionable bar**. Com um sentido parecido com **fashionable** é empregada a palavra **trendy**. O antônimo de **fashionable** é **out of date** ou **old fashioned**.

UK & US English

American English word / spelling	British English word / spelling	Português
color	colour	cor
fall	autumn	outono
pants	trousers*	calça
had on	was wearing	usava, estava usando

* Em inglês britânico, pode-se chamar calça feminina de **pants** ou **trousers**.

GRAMMAR

Expressing the future

Sue usa diferentes construções para expressar futuro. Para algo mais ou menos espontâneo, emprega a forma **will**:

First I'**ll tell** you about the designs.

Usa-se o **future continuous** para expressar uma atividade ou um hábito futuro.

I know what you'**ll be wearing** a year from now.

Para referir-se a algo que vai ocorrer com toda certeza, seja porque se decidiu assim ou porque há provas (**evidences**), usa-se **be going to** + infinitivo.

Colours **are going to be** bright.

Esta estrutura é empregada para se falar de planos futuros e de coisas que já foram decididas.

I'm going to do some work on my house.
I'm going to relax at home because I've had a very busy week.

7 Responda às perguntas abaixo.

What are you going to do tonight?
What are you going to do tomorrow night?
What are you going to do this weekend?

8 Ouça o fragmento abaixo prestando atenção sobretudo na pronúncia de **going to**. Em seguida, leia-o em voz alta imitando a entonação e a pronúncia.

Juliet: So, what are your plans for the weekend?
Sue: Me, I'm going to do some work on my house. And I'm going to see some friends. What about you guys?
Stuart: I've got some friends from Canada staying, so we're going to do some sightseeing, and show them around – the usual tourist stuff.
Juliet: God, I hate it when friends come to stay and you have to be the tourist guide again! But I'm going to relax at home because I've had a very busy week. I'm absolutely knackered.

CULTURAL note

In the USA, the 1920s was a period of enormous social and technological changes: the cinema, cars, the radio, phonographs, new dances and air travel. Women started to enter university, gained the right to vote in 1920, and entered the **workforce** in large numbers, something that women had **shown** they could do during World War One, when millions of men had left their jobs to join the **armed forces**. Working women needed practical, **everyday clothes**. Clothes that could be **washed** easily, clothes that let women move easily, clothes that could be **mass produced** and were inexpensive to buy. Not only clothes: also **bags**, **belts**, **shoes** and **hats**. It was a prosperous period in the economy and a revolution in the clothing industry. The 20s was the decade when fashion entered the modern era, especially for women. It was the decade when women first liberated themselves from constricting fashions and began to wear more comfortable clothes (like short skirts or pants/trousers). For the first time, mobility and **motion** were the most important factors in women's clothes. Women were, for the first time, free to move.

Glossary

armed forces: forças armadas
bag: bolsa
belt: cinto
constricting: limitado
everyday clothes: roupa para o dia a dia
gain (to): ganhar, conseguir
hat: chapéu
mass production: produção em série
motion: movimento
show (to): mostrar
workforce: mão de obra
wash (to): lavar

Take-away English

What do you mean by *young*? ("O que você quer dizer com *jovem*?") é uma forma muito habitual de questionar algo que alguém acaba de dizer ou de pedir um esclarecimento. Por exemplo: **What do you mean by that?** ("O que você quer dizer com isso?"), **What do you mean by** *rationalise*? ("O que você quer dizer com racionalizar?")

You can count on it ("Você pode contar com isso") é uma expressão muito habitual. Outros exemplos: **You can count on us** ("Pode contar conosco"), **Can I count on your support?** ("Posso contar com seu apoio?").

A expressão **out of this world** significa "alucinante", "incrível" etc.

In this day and age ("hoje em dia") é empregado sobretudo para expressar surpresa: **Do you still write letters with a pen and paper in this day and age?**

Of course ("claro", "evidentemente", "sem dúvida") é tão frequente em inglês quanto em português. É muito utilizado em respostas como **Of course I do** ("Claro que sim"), **Of course you can** ("Claro que você pode") etc.

I'm pleased to hear it! ("Fico contente em saber isso", literalmente "Me alegra ouvir isso") também existe em combinações como **I'm delighted to hear that** ou **We're sorry to hear that**.

Sue diz **depending on the climate** ("dependendo do clima"). A estrutura mais habitual é **It depends on...** ("Depende de..."): **It depends on you** ("Depende de você"), **It depends on the economic conditions** ("Depende das condições econômicas").

Glossary

around	em torno de	finished	acabado/a
autumn (UK)	outono	garment	peça (de roupa)
bargain	pechincha	glad	feliz
black	preto/a	green	verde
blue	azul	grey	cinza
bold	audaz, atrevido/a	grow up (to)	crescer
bright	vivo/a, forte	guy	cara *(informal)*
brown	marrom	hate (to)	odiar
busy	ocupado/a	industry	indústria
buy (to)	comprar	inexpensive	econômico/a
casual	informal *(roupa)*	influenced by	influenciado por
charcoal	carvão	knackered	exausto
cheap	barato/a	leggings	calça legging
climate	clima	light	claro/a
clothes	roupas	lightweight	leve, claro/a
colour (UK)		long-sleeve	manga longa
color (US)	cor	mixed	mesclado/a, misturado/a
cotton	algodão	on air	no ar
country house	casa de campo	orange	laranja
cut!	corta!	personally	pessoalmente
dark	escuro/a	poor quality	baixa qualidade
design	desenho, modelo	powerful	potente
design (to)	desenhar	printed	estampado
down	baixo/a	purple	lilás
dress	vestido	rag	trapo, farrapo
easy	fácil	range	gama, variedade
expensive	caro	red	vermelho/a
fabric	tela, tecido	relax (to)	relaxar
fall (US)	outono	retail	varejo (vender no)
fine	fino/a	sale	venda

shade	sombra, tom, matiz	(one) third	um terço *(fração)*
shop	loja	trousers (UK)	calças
short	curto/a	tunic	túnica
show someone around (to)	mostrar a alguém arredores (da cidade)	underneath	(por) debaixo
sightseeing	fazer turismo	unusual	raro/a, incomum
sleeve	manga (de camisa)	variety	variedade
soft	suave	wear	usar, vestir
style	estilo	weekend	fim de semana
subtle	sutil	white	branco/a
suggest (to)	sugerir, indicar	winter	inverno
		wool	lã

Transcript

Stuart: Sue, you're involved in the fashion industry, aren't you?
Sue: Well, yes. I am actually.
St: And is it true that the clothes industry designs and makes clothes a year in advance?
S: Yes, it is. I know what you'll be wearing a year from now.
St: But I don't change my clothes much, I mean, what I mean is – personally I'm not very influenced by trends in fashion.
S: More than you think, Stuart, even you.
Juliet: Maybe you don't know Stuart as well as I do, Sue. Anyway, can you tell us what women will be wearing a year from now.
S: Well, young women –
J: What do you mean by *young*?
S: In the fashion world, young means 18 to 35 years old. First I'll tell you about the designs. So, the new autumn – winter season designs will be very urban, and basically they will be very urban chic and urban casual. You won't get a country house look.
J: So does that mean I won't be going out to my country house next autumn or winter?

S: I'm afraid not. You're going to stay at home all autumn and winter. No country houses for you. You can go out in spring and summer.
J: And will you tell us what to wear then?
S: You can count on it, Jules.
St: And are you going to tell us about colours for the fall and winter?
J: Fall?
St: Where I grew up we say *fall*, but I know you say *autumn*.
S: In the fashion industry we say both. Okay, let me tell you about colours. Good question. Colours are going to be bright, very bright, much brighter than usual, and with a lot of variety of colour, and the designs – the designs are just out of this world! They're going to be printed designs, really bold and powerful printed patterns, and they'll have an Asian look.
J: Asian, you mean Chinese?
S: Well, Asian including China, but also including designs that look Indonesian, Thai, Malaysian, Japanese, even Indian.
St: Are you talking about dresses, trousers or what?

S: Mostly dresses and tunics. They'll be very well designed, to be worn alone or with leggings or pants, or combined with a lightweight long-sleeve polo or top underneath.
St: Long *and* short sleeves?
S: Yes, depending on the climate.
J: And what about colours?
S: We'll be wearing dark green and purple, red mixed with brown –
J: Red with brown? That's an unusual combination.
S: Yes, and combinations of blue and orange.
St: No grey or black?
S: There will be a range of different greys, from light grey to charcoal grey.
St: I'm pleased to hear it!
S: We *are* talking about women's clothes here, Stuart.
J: In the 18 to 35 year old range.
S: Yes. But even the greys will have very bold prints, in contrasting white or dark shades. And the fabric will be mainly synthetic – not very much cotton – but it will be good quality synthetic, and apart from that, about one third of the collection will be wool, very fine, very soft wool.
St: And will the current economic situation be reflected in next year's collection?
S: I'm glad you asked that. Because of this economic crisis, which is happening in the fashion sector too, oh yes, this new collection will be inexpensive and it will be easy to wear. I mean, if it isn't inexpensive, sales will be down.
St: So we'll see cheaper prices?
S: Well, we don't like to use the word cheap, because –
St: it suggests poor quality –
S: Exactly, and we're very sensitive to that in the fashion world, so, for the retail customer, you and me going to the shop to buy garments, the prices for most garments will be around 25 to 35 euros, which is not expensive.
J: No. Not at all.
S: Of course, wool products, dresses, tunics, accessories, will be a little bit more expensive, but that's normal –
J: That's normal, isn't it?
S: But I think to the customer the price represents a real bargain, and a bargain with style. 25 to 35 euros is not expensive at all in this day and age.
J: Well thanks a lot for that, Sue.
St: Yeah, yeah – that was great.
S: You're welcome. Okay, we're finished, aren't we?
J: Yeah – I think so. So, what are your plans for the weekend?
S: Me, I'm going to do some work on my house. And I'm going to see some friends. What about you guys?
St: I've got some friends from Canada staying, so we're going to do some sightseeing, and show them around. You know – the usual tourist stuff.
J: God, I hate it when friends come to stay and you have to be the tourist guide again! But I'm going to relax at home because I've had a very busy week. I'm absolutely knackered.
S: Me too. I'm totally –
Producer: Guys – you're still on air!
J: Oh sorry. Are we finished now?
P: Yes. Cut!

LANGUAGE COMMENTARY 1
TRACK 06 ◀ CD 2

Brian: Bom, Maria, tudo certo até aqui?
Maria: Tenho uma dúvida sobre o *have got*.
B: Diga.
M: É sempre *have got* e não *have*?
B: Bom, o *have* sozinho é muito formal, ao menos para o inglês britânico, ainda que seja usado com maior frequência no inglês norte-americano. Como Martin Luther King, *I have a dream*. Ou seja, para dizer "ter", usa-se *have got* no inglês britânico e *have* no americano.
M: E... *I've, we've* etc.
B: *I've, we've... Contractions*, são as contrações. Pode usar em conversas, cartas informais, cartões-postais, e-mails, entre colegas etc. Principalmente em afirmações e negações, não tanto em perguntas.
M: Certo, e *what do you do?* é usado para perguntar sobre trabalho, né?
B: Se quero saber qual é sua profissão: *What do you do? I'm an electrician, I'm a taxi driver, I'm a biologist* etc.
M: Bem. E os nomes para carne?
B: *Chicken, pork, lamb...*
M: *Lamb* se pronuncia /lam/?
B: Sim, o *b*, nesse caso, quase não se pronuncia. Que mais? *Venison*, que é "veado"; *veal*, que é...
M: "Vitela".
B: *Yes. Beef, turkey*, que é "peru".
M: Mas *Turkey* não é um país?
B: Sim, porque os primeiros perus teriam supostamente vindo da Turquia. Mas, até aí, em português se diz Peru, que é o nome de outro país.
M: Mas é verdade essa história de Turquia?
B: Parece que não. Foram trazidos para a Inglaterra por mercadores portugueses que vinham do que chamavam de Nova Guiné, que eram as Américas, e tudo que era exótico na época acabava recebendo nome de Turquia, Índia...
M: E para que se usa *a bit*?
B: *A bit* é o jeito mais comum de dizer "um pouco". *I'm a bit tired*, "Estou um pouco cansado". "Me dê um pedaço de queijo", *Give me a bit of cheese, please*.
M: O *please* é muito importante para vocês.
B: Sim. Os brasileiros são muito diretos. O português dos portugueses é mais cortês nesse sentido, mas o *please, thank you, excuse me* são imprescindíveis em inglês. Pega muito mal se você não disser *please, thank you, excuse me, sorry*. É falta de educação. Que mais?
M: Os verbos são estranhos.
B: Mudam uma vez, quando chega na terceira pessoa do singular - *he, she, it* - do presente. Você sabe que *sleep* é "dormir". *I sleep, you sleep, he/she/it sleeps, we sleep, you sleep, they sleep*. Por isso, é superimportante dizer o pronome.
M: Senão não se sabe quem fala: eu, tu, você, nós, vós, vocês ou eles.
B: Sim, e a única exceção é o verbo *be*, que muda três vezes: *I am, you are, he/she/it is, we are, you are, they are*. Repare que este é o verbo mais irregular do inglês e somente muda três vezes. Em português eu tenho que aprender seis palavras diferentes.
M: Tenho um pouco de dificuldade com os adjetivos em inglês.
B: Mas eles são muito mais fáceis do que em português! A primeira regra é que eles sempre vêm antes do substantivo. Na entrevista, a Tunde disse: *amazing hotels, special treatment, a large hotel, a normal guest, new hotels*, etc. etc. Certo? Segunda regra: eles não flexionam. *Black* é sempre *black*. *Black* corresponde a "negro", "negra", "negros", "negras". Significa "preto", "preta", "pretos", "pretas". Para vocês os adjetivos em inglês não poderiam ser mais fáceis. Vamos adiante?
M: Claro.

LANGUAGE COMMENTARY 2
TRACK 07 ◀ CD 2

Brian: Fizemos uma apresentação do *past simple*, vimos *would like*, preposições de lugar e um monte de palavras novas. Como está para você, Maria?
Maria: Bem, o *simple past* é tão fácil que nem dá para acreditar. Os verbos não flexionam para nada. *I went, you went, he went, we went, you went, they went*.
B: A única exceção é o passado de *be*: *I was, you were, he/she/it was, we were, you were, they were*. E as perguntas do tipo *yes/no* começam com *did, could, was, were*. Como em *Did you remember to buy fruit?* Ou *Did Keith talk to you?* E com o *was/were* não é preciso usar outro verbo. *Was Duncan at the meeting? Were you at home last night? Were your children with you?*
M: Eu vi que, se o verbo não muda, é importante colocar o pronome na frente.
B: Sim. Em português, "fomos" necessariamente é "nós fomos", não pode ser outra coisa, mas *went* pode ser qualquer pessoa, ao menos se não houver contexto. É claro que se o sujeito for o mesmo que antes, não é preciso repetir.
M: Claro. Bem, pronúncia. *Walk* e *work*, "andar" e "trabalhar", para mim é difícil diferenciar um do outro.

B: Entendo. São pronunciados da mesma forma, menos a vogal. E ambas as vogais são longas: /ó/ and /ô/. *Walk* and *work*. Você ouve a diferença? /ó/, /ô/, *walk*, *work*. Percebe a diferença?
M: Sim, sim, claro.
B: Pode praticar uma frase bem simples. *I walk to work*, "Vou andando para o trabalho". *I walk to work. Say it.*
M: *I walk to work.*
B: *Walk work. I walk to work.*
M: *I walk to work.*
B: *Good. Now practice a hundred times before tomorrow*. Alguma outra dúvida?
M: *Would like* é um pouco estranho.
B: Em que sentido?
M: A pronúncia principalmente, mas se usa para pedir uma coisa de um jeito *polite* e também para expressar o que você quer fazer, não?
B: Podem te perguntar em uma loja: *How would you like to pay? I'd like to pay by credit card*. E quando não há um verbo, como *pay*, mas uma coisa, fica: *Would you like some ham?*
M: E a pronúncia?
B: É empregada a forma com contração em afirmações e em negações: *I'd like, We'd like, You'd like, I wouldn't like*, etc. *I wouldn't like to offend you*. Se pronuncia como *wood*, de "madeira", e se acrescenta *ent*: *wouldn't*. Esqueça o *l* completamente. São frases bem comuns em inglês.
M: Ok. E a pronúncia dos verbos regulares?
B: A terminação, você quer dizer? É /d/: *impress, impressed, phone, phoned*, com as consonantes suaves. Mas ele soa como /t/ depois de consonantes como /k/ ou /p/ como *walked, worked, stopped*. E soa como... /id/ se o verbo termina em d, t, u ou y. *I posted a letter, posted, I needed a drink, I fancied a drink*, "Eu gostaria de uma bebida".
M: Bem. No caso dos comparativos, você tem que pensar se o adjetivo é de uma, duas ou três sílabas. É assim, não?
B: Sim, a regra básica é essa: *one syllable, add -er*, por exemplo, *bigger, better, faster, whiter*. Se forem duas, é preciso juntar o *more* sem alterar o adjetivo: *more decent*, "mais decente", *more formal*. Ou *less* se for o caso de usar "menos". *This is less common than* não sei o quê.
M: Mas...
B: Mas?
M: Se terminar em *y*, é como se fosse de uma sílaba, não?
B: É muito fácil pensar em *sexy*. *Gisele Bündchen is sexier than Hebe Camargo*. Ou *Wagner Moura is sexier than...*
M: Gisele Bündchen.
B: Tá, tá. E na parte que fala de Maria Elena, a nova-iorquina?

M: Ficou claro, mas percebi que o gerúndio é muito usado.
B: Sim, sim, sim. Principalmente se o verbo for o sujeito da frase. *Smoking is bad for you*. Ou o objeto: *The important thing is brushing correctly*. Ou depois de uma preposição: *Instead of helping*, "em vez de ajudar", ou depois de *like, dislike, love, hate*, etc. *I love watching the rain*, "Eu adoro contemplar a chuva".
M: Bom, preciso praticar. Essa parte não é tão fácil para mim.
B: Sim. E fique esperta quando ouvir ou ver isso, combinado?
M: Combinado.

LANGUAGE COMMENTARY 3
TRACK 08 ◀CD 2
M: Bem, vejo que tenho três coisas para perguntar aqui sobre gramática, além de bastante vocabulário.
B: Pode falar. Estou ouvindo.
M: Primeiro, a parte das receitas, que é basicamente com verbos no imperativo, não?
B: Isso mesmo. E o que você notou sobre o imperativo em inglês?
M: Que é muito simples.
B: É claro, só há uma única forma, que é...
M: É como o infinitivo, mas sem o *to* antes, não é? E não existe diferença entre "você" e "tu".
B: Perfeito. Porque em inglês não existem dois pronomes diferentes para a segunda pessoa.
M: Nem no singular nem no plural. É tudo igual.
B: Sim, sim. *Cook, grill, roast, eat*, etc.
M: Mas, Brian, às vezes você usa o *you* antes.
B: Sim, como *First you grill the aubergines*. Ou seja, em um livro de receitas o imperativo apareceria sempre sozinho, mas, quando você está explicando a uma pessoa, a um amigo, você pode dirigir a frase a ele, introduzindo o *you*: *First you chop the potatoes, then you beat the eggs*, etc. Bastante fácil, não?
M: Preciso admitir que sim.
B: Quando nós aprendemos o português precisamos aprender duas formas do imperativo, e as flexões podem variar muito de acordo com o verbo. Em inglês só há uma forma, não tem erro. Que mais?
M: Tenho que estudar muito o vocabulário que tem a ver com cozinha, tanto os verbos, como *fry, boil, grill*, quanto a comida.
B: Está certo, Maria, mas a maioria desses verbos se parece com o português: *fry*, "fritar", *cut*, "cortar", *serve*, "servir", e dá para reconhecer muito do vocabulário de comida também, como nomes das frutas, das verduras, das carnes, dos peixes.

M: E como se diz "caipirinha" em inglês?
B: Se diz /caipirinha/, assim mesmo. Mas se escreve igual.
M: Além disso, "prato" não é *plate*, não é?
B: Não, *plate* é o que você lava na pia, um *plate* é feito de cerâmica, mas um prato de comida é um *dish*, como *What's your favourite dish?* Bem, e o passado, *the past simple?*
M: Outra coisa que achei superfácil. Só há uma palavra para todas as pessoas.
B: Exceto o passado de *to be*, que tem duas, *was* e *were*. *I was, you were, he/she/it was, we were, you were, they were.* E normalmente se fala muito suave, como *I was here, We were there.* Isso se chama *weak form*, forma suave ou fraca. E as perguntas tipo *yes/no?*
M: Quer dizer que a resposta sempre será "sim" ou "não", correto?
B: Sim, por isso essas perguntas começam com um verbo auxiliar, *was* ou *were*, *could*, mas o mais frequente é *did: Did you see the match last night? Did she go to university?* E o verbo principal sempre na forma do infinitivo, mas sem o *to*. *Did Bob say that? Did Simon arrive on time?*
M: Certo, certo. Aí não tem segredo, mas as perguntas com *what, who, where, when* etc. são mais complicadas, não?
B: Creio que sim. São *wh- questions: who, which, what* etc., além de *how, how much, how many, how long*, que em termos de gramática também fazem parte desta categoria.
M: É que não ficou tão claro para mim quando devo usar o *did* nesse tipo de pergunta.
B: Bem, se sabemos que em uma partida de futebol a Alemanha perdeu de 1 a 0, mas não sabemos quem venceu os alemães, perguntamos: *Who beat Germany?* Ou seja, sabemos o verbo, *beat*, que é "derrotar", e sabemos o objeto direto, Alemanha, mas não sabemos o sujeito do verbo. No caso, o verbo auxiliar não é necessário, é só dizer *Who beat Germany?* E a resposta? Pode ser *Brazil, Brazil beat Germany* ou apenas *Brazil did*.
M: Então a gente usa *did* quando não sabe o objeto?
B: Exatamente. *Who did Brazil beat?* Vemos os brasileiros pulando e agitando as bandeiras, mas não sabemos o objeto, neste caso, do verbo *beat*. E a resposta seria: *Germany, They beat Germany* ou *We beat Germany*, se você for brasileiro, ou *Brazil beat Germany.*
M: Me dê outro exemplo.
B: *How many medals did the USA win at the Beijing Olympics?* Resposta?
M: Como é que eu vou saber?
B: Bem, sabemos que os norte-americanos ganharam muitas medalhas, mas não sabemos *how many?*, "Quantas": *How many medals did the USA win?* Bom, ganharam 110. *They won 110 medals.* Mas vamos pegar outro caso: sabemos que um país ganhou 15 medalhas em Beijing em 2008. A pergunta nesse caso seria: *Who won 15 medals?*
M: O Brasil!
B: Isso! Percebe que a resposta tem a ver com o sujeito? *Brazil, Brazil won 15 medals.* E se você quiser saber quantas medalhas ganhou a Austrália?
M: *How many medals did Australia win?*
B: *46, Australia won 46 medals.*
M: 46?
B: Sim, foi um ano ruim para a Austrália. Agora, falando de esporte, na unidade sobre grandes momentos da história do esporte, vimos *the present perfect*. Aqui há três funções: tempo muito recente, como notícias: *Something has happened* ou *Something has just happened*, "Algo acaba de acontecer". O inglês usa o *present perfect*, *have* ou *has* com o particípio passado, quando em português se emprega o presente, presente do indicativo.
M: Ou seja, não é como o pretérito perfeito em português?
B: Sua forma é parecida, mas não corresponde necessariamente ao *present perfect* inglês em dois dos três conceitos do *present perfect*. Não corresponde ao conceito de *indefinite time*, do tempo indefinido. Dizemos "Ele esteve no Japão?", no pretérito perfeito simples, quando em inglês seria...?
M: *Have you been in Japan?*
B: Quase, quase. *Have you been to Japan?* ou *Have you ever been to Japan?* Também é diferente quando falamos que algo "É o mais não sei o quê que eu vi ou provei na minha vida". *It's the most interesting film that I've ever seen.*
M: Agora qual é o terceiro uso do *present perfect*, o que corresponde ao pretérito perfeito composto?
B: É o que chamamos *continuing time*. Algo que começou no passado e continua no presente. E isso é feito com *how long*, sobretudo quando se trata de uma pergunta. É um...
M: Calma, calma. Este *How long* é para tempo ou distância?
B: Bem, tempo, como "durante quanto tempo" ou "desde quando", melhor dizendo, mas também serve para questões de geografia, como *How long is the Amazon River?* E o tal do *continuing time* é usado com *since* e *for*. *I've been studying this subject for six months*, "Tenho estudado esse assunto nos últimos seis meses". *I've been here for ten years.* Ou: *We've had this car since 2004.*
M: E não se pode dizer *I am here for ten years?*

LANGUAGE COMMENTARY

B: Não, a não ser que a intenção seja dizer algo como "Minha permanência aqui será de dez anos", "Vou passar dez anos aqui". Que mais? *Since* se usa para "desde quando", estabelecendo quando se iniciou o estado ou a ação, como *They've been married since 1995*.
M: Estão casados desde 1995?
B: Sim, e *since* é desde um ponto no tempo: *since 1976, since September the 11th, since Monday; since 10 o'clock*. Sempre o ponto de partida. Enquanto *for* expressa a duração do estado ou da ação: *for ten minutes, for five days, for two years*.
M: Sempre um número, não?
B: Praticamente. Agora, a voz passiva, *the passive voice*.
M: Me parece que a forma do verbo "ser", ou seja, *to be*, com o particípio passado, é igual ao português.
B: Sim. "A exposição foi inaugurada pelo Ministro da Cultura", *The exhibition was opened by the Minister of Culture*, ainda que seja possível usar *got* no lugar de *be*, pelo menos em situações informais. Acho que o que se deve levar em conta aqui é que se usa muito a voz passiva em inglês, assim como em português, "O quadro foi vendido por 100 mil euros", *The painting was sold for 100,000 euros*. É bem parecido, não?
M: Pois é. É bem claro. Deixe-me ver a unidade outra vez, ok?

LANGUAGE COMMENTARY 4
TRACK 09 ◀CD 2

M: Tenho uma pergunta para você, senhor Brian.
B: Sou todo ouvidos.
M: *Get*. O que quer dizer *get*?
B: Você se refere à entrevista com a Gemma, não é verdade?
M: Exatamente.
B: Bem, vimos que *get* tem muitos significados e existe em centenas de combinações. Mas o principal é "conseguir", "obter", "receber", como *Today I got an email from my ex*.
M: "Hoje eu recebi um e-mail do meu ex". Mas não se pode dizer *Today I received...*
B: Sim, sim, é possível também. Mas *get* soa bem mais natural.
M: "Recebi um presente?"
B: *I got a present*. Também *I got a mobile phone for my birthday, My daughter got some new shoes, My mother got a camera, We got some information*.
M: E os outros usos do *get*?
B: *Get* + adjetivo é como *become*, "tornar-se", "ficar": *get hungry, get angry, get depressed, get excited, get tired, get interested. Get* + lugar é "chegar": *get home, get to university; get to work, get to Juazeiro do Norte*. E muitas coisas que em português são verbos reflexivos, ou seja, com "se", em inglês são combinações com *get*: "vestir-se", *get dressed*, "despir-se", *get undressed*, "levanta-se", *get up*.
M: E o passado é sempre *got*?
B: Sim, *got engaged, got married, got separated, got divorced*.
M: Percebo que com o *get* você vai para qualquer lugar.
B: Correto. E o *t* se junta com a vogal seguinte na hora de pronunciar: *get angry, get up, get on*.
M: *Get on* você não me ensinou.
B: "Dar-se bem". *She gets on well with her classmates*.
M: "Ele se dá bem com seus companheiros de classe", não?
B: Muito bem.
M: Outra coisa. O futuro se faz com *will*.
B: O inglês não tem um futuro simples como em português, francês, italiano ou espanhol. O mais simples é *will*, mas *will* se usa para muitas outras coisas. *Will* é comum com *I think, I say, I believe* e seus negativos, certo? Suas negações, e para descrever algo certo, programado: *A car will meet you at the airport, Your plane will arrive at Guarulhos not Congonhas*. Emprega-se *going to, be going to*, para prever o futuro, para falar de seus planos pessoais, e quando você tem uma prova ou algo que indica o que vai acontecer, talvez por convicção pessoal ou por evidências: *Oh look at those clouds!* ("Veja essas nuvens") *It's going to rain* ("Vai chover"), *You're going to have problems with that boy* ("Você vai ter problemas com esse menino").
M: Algo mais?
B: Sim, sim, sim, mas fica para daqui a pouco...
M: Há muito vocabulário para caráter e comportamento.
B: É verdade, mas considere que metade do vocabulário do inglês vem das mesmas raízes latinas e gregas, assim como o português. Quero dizer que metade do vocabulário do inglês é dada de presente. Por exemplo, na unidade dos horóscopos – *horoscopes* –, você viu *dogmatic, enthusiastic, protective, perfectionism, focus, friction*, e muito, muito mais.
M: Bem, Brian, e as *question tags*?
B: *Isn't it? Are you? Did they? Will she?*
M: Sim, mas tenho que pensar muito.
B: Você pode fazer pequenos diálogos ou converter afirmações em perguntas, como *Susana comes from Lisbon, doesn't she?* ou *Anna went to Bogotá, didn't she?* Sei que isso é mais complicado que pôr sempre "não?" ou "não é?" no final da frase, mas as *question tags* são importantes porque são muito frequentes. Na verdade, são 25% de todas as perguntas em interação oral em inglês.
M: Mais uma pergunta: *cell phone* e *mobile phone* significam a mesma coisa?

B: Se diz *cell phone* nos Estados Unidos, Austrália e Nova Zelândia e *mobile phone* na Inglaterra e na Irlanda. Mas o mesmo acontece entre o português de Portugal e o do Brasil, com "celular" neste e "móvel" ou "telemóvel" naquele.
M: Sim, acho que sim.

LANGUAGE COMMENTARY 5
TRACK 10 ◀ CD 2

M: Gostei muito da unidade *First love*.
B: E por quê?
M: Porque são experiências quase universais. Quer dizer, se você tiver a sorte de viver em uma sociedade livre e moderna, não é? Gostei do vocabulário, mas não entendi bem a diferença entre *a crush* e *infatuation*.
B: *Okay, to have a crush on somebody* é bem adolescente. Muitas vezes é um segredo, talvez o objeto do amor sequer se dê conta, quem sabe porque não é correspondido, mas é um amor bastante unidirecional, portanto, não acontece nada. Frequentemente, diz-se *a schoolboy crush* ou a *schoolgirl crush*, que era precisamente o caso de Juliet. *Infatuation. To be infatuated with somebody* é bem parecido, mas não é sempre juvenil. Sempre tem, isso sim, um aspecto um pouco ridículo ou extravagante, como uma paixão louca de um homem mais velho por uma bailarina jovem etc.
M: Mas por que se diz *fall in love*?
B: *Falling in love again, never wanted to...* Bom, suponho que é como uma queda, não? Você perde o equilíbrio...
M: E o passado é *felt in love*?
B: No, *felt* é o passado de *feel*, que é "sentir". O passado de *fall* é *fell*.
M: A Juliet disse *He asked me out*. Isso é como "perguntar-me fora"?
B: Essa seria uma tradução literal e equivocada. Na realidade, é mais como "Ele me pediu para sair com ele". Porque *ask* é "perguntar", mas também "pedir". *to ask somebody out* é, numa situação romântica, convidar alguém para sair. Pedir a mão de alguém é *to ask for somebody's hand*.
M: Ok. Agora, o *past continuous*. É usado para situar a história, no tempo e em um lugar, correto?
B: É isso mesmo. Como diz Stuart na unidade, *We were living in Indonesia;* Juliet diz *I was looking for a job*. Não são os pontos específicos do relato, mas o contexto.
M: Sim, claro. Muito bem. Os dois rapazes falam de como se dão com seus pais, e aparecem umas expressões um pouco complicadas, como alguns *phrasal verbs*.
B: E?
M: São importantes?
B: São verbos usados o tempo todo. É importante você aprender! Mais cedo ou mais tarde, você vai ter que dominá-los, como "ser" e "estar" em português. Anote em uma caderneta.
M: Tá bom, tá bom. Farei isso. Também gostei da unidade sobre a moda, mas há muito vocabulário de roupa.
B: Por que você não vai nomeando? Diga os nomes das peças que você veste pela manhã em inglês. Anote as coisas que não sabe e depois as procure durante o dia em um dicionário. Assim, quando você estiver fazendo compras em Nova Iorque ou Londres ou Berlim ou Singapura, já terá todo o vocabulário.
M: Ah, ok, ok. Com certeza. E a palavra *fashion*? Aqui dizemos que algo ou alguém "é muito fashion". Está correto?
B: Não, Maria. Isso é mistura do inglês com o português. *Fashion* é um substantivo, um *noun*, que pode estar acompanhado de um adjetivo, como em *a fashion show, the fashion business;* mas, para dizer que uma coisa está na moda, é *fashionable*. *Fashionable*.
M: *Fashionable*.
B: *Opposite?*
M: *Not fashionable?*
B: Maria!
M: *Unfashionable*.
B: *Much better*.
M: Certo. A diferença entre *printed* e *designs*?
B: *Printed* é literalmente "impresso" ou "estampado". *Design* é qualquer tipo de modelo ou padrão, como riscos, pontos, ou sem nada.
M: Ok. E, para terminar, existe alguma diferença entre *I've played* e *I've been playing*?
B: *I've played* indica algo terminado, enquanto *I've been playing* é uma atividade que pode ser retomada ou algo que alguém continua fazendo. É preciso prestar bastante atenção no sentido do verbo. De qualquer modo, tudo é vocabulário, e as palavras são os elementos que levam o significado, e as palavras têm sua gramática internamente, como o código genético do DNA... Você não acha que...? Maria, está me ouvindo?
M: Hein?

ANSWER KEY

TRACK 01 CD 1

1 1. your job, 2. holidays, 3. recent holidays, 4. life in different places, 5. food, 6. interview with a dental hygienist, 7. music, 8. sport, 9. horoscopes, 10. quiz, 11. teenagers, 12. phone-in selling, 13. weddings

2 1 c, 2 b, c, d, e 3 e 4 e, 5 d

3 How are **you** today? (descendente)
And what's **that** about? (descendente)
And **then**? (ascendente)
Your favourite **food**? (ascendente)
Is that the same as a **dentist**? (ascendente)
And **what's** the quiz about? (descendente)
With your **parents** or your **children**? (descendente)
So is that **it** for **today**? (ascendente)

4 **Feminine:** wife, sister, mother, girlfriend, daughter / **Fem. or masc.:** parents, children, partner / **Masculine:** husband, brother, boyfriend, son, father

5 **Feminine:** grandmother, aunt, niece, granddaughter / **Fem. or masc.:** cousin, grandchildren, grandparents / **Masculine:** uncle, nephew, grandfather, grandson

6 1. husband, 2. daughter, son and children, 3. sister, 4. girlfriend, 5. uncle and aunt, 6. grandchildren

7 1. We**'ve got / have got**...
2. ... **has** your brother **got**?
He**'s got / has got** five
3. **Has** your sister got a boyfriend?
... I **haven't got** a girlfriend, okay?
4. Stuart **'s got / has got** a Canadian accent.
5. Yes, I think I**'ve got / have got** more than 400. But **have** you **got** time to listen to them?
6. **Has** the USA got 52 states?
I really **haven't got** any idea.
7. I **haven't got** any time.
... you **'ve got / have got** a Physics exam.
8. **Have** you got a car?
Yes, I **'ve got / have got** a Renault Megane.
9. Argentina **have** normally **got** a very good...
10. Simon **'s got / has got** long hair in this one!

8

Sing. sub. pronoun	Sing. possessive	Sing. obj. pronoun
I (eu)	**my** (meu/meus/ minha/minhas)	**me** (me, mim)
you (tu,você)	**your** (teu/tua, seu/sua)	**you** (te, ti, se, o, a, lhe)
he (ele)	**his** (seu, dele)	**him** (o, lhe, se)
she (ela)	**her** (sua, dela)	**her** (a, lhe, se)
it (ele, ela)	**its** (seu, dele)	**it** (o, a, se, lhe)
Pl. sub. pronoun	Pl. possessive	Pl. obj. pronoun
we (nós)	**our** (nosso/ nossa)	**us** (nos)
you (vocês)	**your** (seus, de vocês)	**you** (os, as, lhes, se)
they (eles/elas)	**their** (seus/suas, deles/delas)	**them** (os, as, lhes, se)

TRACK 02 CD 1

1 What is Dean's job?

2 1 b, 2 a, 3 c, 4 d

3 What does Tunde do?

4 1 c, 2 b, 3 b, 4 c

5 beef novilho   ostrich avestruz
chicken frango   pork (carne de) porco
goat cabrito   rabbit coelho
kangaroo canguru   turkey peru
lamb cordeiro   venison veado (cervo)

6 beef, kangaroo, lamb, venison

7 1. False: she contacts them / 2. True / 3. True. 4. False: bigger than now. / 5. True.

8 **Well**, first I check the **web**sites of the **new** hotels I want to **vis**it in a certain **area**, and **then** I **call** them to make an ap**point**ment. **Next**, I **fol**low that up with an em**ail** and I also email all our participating hotels in that area to make appointments with them, too.

9 **work:** 1st person sing., **is:** 3rd person sing.
are: 3rd person pl., **are:** 3rd person pl.
offer: 3rd person pl., **know:** 2nd person sing.
want: 3rd person pl., **does:** 3rd person sing.
attracts: 3rd person sing., **travels:** 3rd person sing.

10 tercera / singular / **s**

11 comes, lives, teaches, works, drives, takes, works, prepares, studies, starts, goes

12

1) Yes / No questions	2) Information / Explanation answer
Do you travel much in your job?	Who do you sell to?
Do they give you special treatment?	Who do you work for?
Do you like your job?	What does your work involve?
Do you ever get tired of travelling?	What do you mean?

1) **Do / Does.** / Subject pronoun or name. / Infinitive without **to**.
2) **Wh-** question word. / Auxiliary verb **do** (or other). / Infinitive without **to**.

13 1. Where do the children play? / 2. Who is that girl? 3. Do you smoke? / 4. Can she speak Basque? 5. Why does this happen? / 6. Where do you live ? / 7. Do you like Salvador Dalí? / 8. Does your sister play football? / 9. Do you come from Caracas?

TRACK 03 CD 1

1 Sue: The Seychelles, The Maldives / Juliet: Costa Rica / Stuart: Nepal

2 Sue: 4 / Juliet: 2, 5, 6, 9, 11 / Stuart: 1, 7, 8 / Nobody: 3, 10

3 I **want** to **talk** about **hol**idays. /wontutork/
I **love** holidays, when I can **get** them. /kungethem/

154   ANSWER KEY

But I **think** that's the **same** for **everyone**. /furevriwon/

Now I **want** to ask you **both** a question about **hol**idays. /wantuwaskyu/

4 dream sonho, ideal / cultural cultural / mountain montanha / exclusive exclusivo / peace paz / beautiful bonito / beach praia / expensive caro / tourism turismo / clean limpo/a / destination destino / interesting interessante / holiday férias / dependent on que vive de / vegetation vegetação / walk caminhar / island ilha / swim nadar / water água / silence silêncio / place lugar

5 tourism, islands, holidays, beach, destinations, beautiful, dependent, clean, swim / cultural, mountains, silence, walk / expensive, place, exclusive, water, vegetation, nature

6 North
West   East
    South

7 1 h, 2 c, 3 g, 4 e, 5 a, 6 h, 7 b, 8 i, 9 f

8 Monday, Tuesday, Wednesday, Thursday, Friday, Saturday, Sunday / January, February, March, April, May, June, July, August, September, October, November, December

9 Sun / Sunday, Moon / Monday, Mars / Tuesday, Wednesday, Quinta / Thursday, Venus / Sexta / Friday, Saturday

10 1 a, 2 c, 3 b, 4 a, 5 b, 6 c, 7 a, 8 c

11 1 b, 2 a, 3 a, 4 b, 5 a, 6 a, 7 b

12 1. Me neither, 2. Me too, 3. Me too, 4. Me too, 5. Me neither, 6. Me neither, 7. Me too, 8. Me neither, 9. Me neither, 10. Me neither

TRACK 04 CD 1

1 Auckland, Manukau, Wellington, Dunedin, Kaikoura, Picton, Queenstown / 1 a, 2 b

2 1. **True** (She mentions this twice) 2. **False** (25%) 3. **True** (They travelled in a campervan and stayed with friends) 4. **False** (They went to two rugby matches) 5. **True** ("lot of extreme sports") 6. **True** ("came up and gave us free tickets") 7. **False** (They had dinner) 8. **False** (familiar, but cooked in different ways) 9. **True** ("very generous")

3 drove, took, mentioned, was, did, had

4 be ▸ **was/were**, can ▸ **could**, take ▸ **took**, see ▸ **saw**, say ▸ **said**, go ▸ **went**, do ▸ **did**, have ▸ **had**, eat ▸ **ate**

5 **Regular:** impressed, rented, stayed, wanted, cooked, liked / **Irregular:** drove, put on, spent, thought

6 went, took, stayed, travelled, didn't have, liked, could, were, saw, gave, didn't need, ate, put on

7 1. If something wasn't as interesting as ... / We couldn't believe it! / Si el auxiliar es también el verbo principal, le añadimos **not**.
2. We didn't have a fixed schedule / She didn't need them / Verbo auxiliar (**did**) + infinitivo SIN **to**
3. Did you sleep in the campervan all the time? / Did you do any kind of cultural activity? / Did you try any new kinds of food? / Verbo auxiliar (**did**) + infinitivo SIN **to**
4. Was it a good experience? / El verbo auxiliar.

8 cooked cozinhar, drove dirigir, put on weight engordar, rented alugar, spent gastar, stayed alojar-se, took tomar/pegar, wanted querer, went ir, saw ver

9 1 b, 2 e, 3 i, 4 d, 5 f, 6 a, 7 c, 8 g, 9 j, 10 h

10 1. could, 2. liked, 3. impressed, 4. gave, 5. thought, 6. had, 7. took, 8. spent, 9. stayed, 10. wanted.

11 1. was, 2. stay, 3. stay, 4. were, 5. was, 6. staying, 7. stay, 8. stay, 9. am, 10. stay.

12 1. stay away, 2. stay out, 3. stay in, 4. stay up

13 went, were, was, was, had, took, saw, were, happened, was, put on, stayed, spent, thought

14 **More in Western Europe:** high population density, tall buildings, high price of food in supermarkets, high price of houses, family-focused people
More in New Zealand: high standard of living, big houses, wet weather, sunny weather, high price of wine, independent people

15

One syllable	Two syllables (**-y**)
cheap, high, dry, thin, sweet, wet, big, small, tall, low, fat, nice, fast, slow	sexy, sunny, happy, heavy, easy, ugly, angry, hungry

Two syllables	Three or four syllables
polite, stupid, complex, boring, simple, helpful	expensive, independent, difficult, populated, beautiful

16 Formas corretas: sunnier, wetter, higher, bigger, less expensive, more expensive, fatter, more independent

17 1 d, 2 b, 3 a, 4 c, 5 e, 6 e

18 **For a place:** cheap, expensive, independent, sunny, nice, ugly, beautiful, boring, wet, dry
For a person: character polite, sweet, stupid, sexy, independent, complex, simple, helpful, nice, easy, difficult, boring, dry
For a person: physical thin, heavy, tall, short, ugly, beautiful
For food: cheap, expensive, sweet, heavy, simple, nice, delicious, easy, difficult, boring

19 ugly - beautiful, cheap - expensive, high - low, easy - difficult, fast - slow, dry - wet (sweet se se trata de vinho), complex - simple, thin - fat

20 1. nicer, 2. cheaper, 3. beautiful, 4. sexier,

5. more difficult, 6. better, 7. sweeter, 8. simpler,
9. drier, 10. more independent

TRACK 05 ◀ CD 1

1 1. They brush their teeth badly. / They don't use the brush correctly. 2. Twice a year. / Every 6 months. 3. She likes seeing people, meeting people, discussing things with people.

2 1. True 2. True (if the technique is wrong) 3. True 4. False (people who have a genetic problem)

3 things, help, about

4 the most important thing / the main thing / our role is... / for one thing... / That's really what it's all about.

5 1 d, 2 e, 3 b, 4 a, 5 c

6 frankly francamente, efficiently eficientemente, effectively acertadamente, regularly com regularidade, often frequentemente, three or four times a day três ou quatro vezes por dia, correctly corretamente, all the time constantemente, properly devidamente, exactly exatamente, normally normalmente, every six months a cada seis meses, twice a year duas vezes por ano, sometimes às vezes

7 **Frequency:** regularly, often, three or four times a day, all the time, normally, every six months, twice a year, sometimes
Manner: efficiently, effectively, correctly, properly
Focusing: frankly, exactly

8 1. every six months / twice a year
2. efficiently / effectively 3. correctly / properly
4. often / regularly 5. three or four times a day
6. frankly 7. efficiently / effectively 8. efficiently / effectively 9. sometimes 10. regularly / often

TRACK 06 ◀ CD 1

1 aubergine c, cucumber l, dill d, garlic k, honey b, mint i, olives f, olive oil h, onion a, pepper e, salt j, watermelon g

2 **Fruit:** watermelon, apple, banana, grape, kiwifruit, lemon, mandarin, melon, peach
Vegetables: aubergine, garlic, onion, cucumber, carrot, lettuce, mushroom, potato, zucchini
Fish & seafood: lobster, mussel, octopus, prawn, salmon, sardine, sole, squid, trout
Meat: bacon, beef, chicken, goat, ham, lamb, pork, turkey, veal **Herbs & spices:** dill, mint, pepper, salt, basil, oregano, parsley, rosemary, thyme **Dairy produce:** butter, cheese, cream, milk, yoghurt **Other:** honey, olives, olive oil, bread, egg, flour, margarine, nuts, pasta

3 descascar peel, misturar mix, cortar (em cubos) chop, fritar fry, servir serve, fatiar slice, gratinar/ralar grate, ferver boil, escorrer drain

4 secar dry, cozinhar cook, pôr/colocar put, combinar combine, acrescentar add, deixar leave, esfriar cool, coar strain, mergulhar dip

5 **Recipe 1:** cucumber, dill, garlic, mint, olives, olive oil, salt, yoghurt
Recipe 2: aubergine, garlic, olive oil, onion, pepper, ricotta cheese, salt, spaghetti, tomatoes
Recipe 3: honey, mint, watermelon, yoghurt

6 **make** the tomato sauce, **add** salt and pepper, **boil** the pasta, **chop** the tomatoes and onion, **slice** the aubergines, **fry** the aubergines

7 peel, chop, put, leave, dry, peel, chop, mix, add, combine, cool

TRACK 07 ◀ CD 1

1 Good (great experience, opened his mind, met a lot of people, saw where his ancestors lived...)
Good: his flat, his work, the people at work, the cities, the parks, public transport, football
Bad: the food, the winters
Not mentioned: the summers, his salary, parties

2 Rob is a pharmacist.

3 1. False: he had it at work 2, 3, 4, 5. True
6. False: he met them after work
7. False: he went to bed at 11.30

4 Newcastle, Dublin, Edinburgh, Durham

5 1. **No**, I **didn't**. I **lived** in **New**castle, in the north**east** of **Eng**land.
2. I **lived** there for nearly **two years**. Then I returned to the **States**.
3. What I **liked** was the **job** that I **had**.
4. What I **didn't** like was the **free**zing, dark **win**ters, and their **food**.
5. In my **free** time I did **lots** of things.
6. I loved **stay**ing at **home** and **read**ing a **book**, or sometimes I **cooked** nice **Mex**ican **food** for my **friends**.

6 cooked, had, thought, wanted, was/were, went

7 1. learned, 2. chose, 3. did/made, 4. did/made, 5. lived, 6. met, 7. gave, 8. emigrated, 9. woke up, 10. finished, 11. became, 12. called/phoned, 13. realised, 14. liked, 15. needed, 16 travelled, 17. watched

8 We add **-d**, **-ed** or **-ied** (Não há nenhum exemplo de -ied)
Regular pasts: called, lived, cooked, needed, emigrated, phoned, finished, realised, learned, travelled, liked, watched
Irregular pasts: became, made, met, chose, thought, did, was/were, gave, went, had, woke up

9 1. did, 2. I did, 3. make, 4. make, 5. do, 6. make, 7. doing, 8. do, 9. doing, 10. do, 11. make
· We normally use **make** for producing, causing...
· We use **do** for indefinite activities.
· We normally use **do** for an action...
· We use **do** when we talk about work, jobs...

10 1. made/cooked, 2. lived, 3. phoned, 4. went, 5. met, 6. made, 7. woke up, 8. realised, 9. gave, 10. became

TRACK 08 CD 1

1 At the 1976 Olympic Games Nadia Comaneci scored a perfect score of 10.
At the 1984 winter Games Torvill and Dean had 12 maximum points from all 12 judges.
At the 1972 Olympic Games Mark Spitz won seven gold medals.
At the 2008 Olympic Games Michael Phelps won eight gold medals.

2 1. Sue 2. Stuart 3. Juliet 4. Stuart, Sue 5. Sue

3 1. Six. 2. The only winter Games in a communist country. 3. Because they became professional. 4. The (artistic beauty and emotion of the) Opening Ceremony.

4 1. interesting, Olympics 2. philosophical, expecting 3. famous 4. titles, gymnastics, perfect 5. professional, compete 6. incredible athletes 7. emotional moment, ceremony

5
athletics	cycling
hockey	motorcycle racing
table-tennis	sailing
boxing	badminton
fencing	tennis
squash	football
archery	gymnastics
judo	wrestling
canoeing	rowing
triathlon	ski-ing
billiards	basketball
rugby	swimming
golf	jogging
weightlifting	diving

6 **play** + badminton, basketball, billiards, football, golf, hockey, rugby, squash, table-tennis, tennis.
They all have a **ball** and...

7 **go** + canoeing, cycling, jogging, rowing, sailing, skiing, swimming / They all end in **-ing** and...

8 a) some time in the past

9 ... the auxiliary verb **have/has** and the **past participle**.

10 1 c, 2 b, 3 c, 4 a, 5 b, 6 a, 7 c, 8 a, 9 c, 10 b
since **c**, just **a**, How long **c**, for **c**, ever **b**

11 ... the auxiliary verb **to be** and the **past participle**.

12 1. are made, 2. were delayed, 3. will be made, 4. has been considered

TRACK 09 CD 1

1 Sue: **Yes**, Stuart: **No**, Brian: **No**, Juliet: **Yes**

2 **Aquarius:** independent, imaginative, unemotional, cool
Pisces: generous, sensitive, secretive, can't focus on the real world
Aries: open, dynamic, impulsive
Taurus: values the family, lives for the people he/she loves, stubborn, possessive
Gemini: energetic, adventurous involved in lots of things, doesn't always finish things
Cancer: trusting, private, protective, overemotional
Leo: enthusiastic, warm, pompous, bossy
Virgo: good in teams, enjoys helping others, too perfectionist, focuses on very small things
Libra: charming, likes balance, too analytical
Scorpio: adaptable, intense, jealous, secretive
Sagittarius: idealistic, optimistic, too direct
Capricorn: patient, responsible, dislikes fantasy

3 1. tended **to**, 2. focus **on**, 3. believe **in**, 4. spent € 1000 **on**

4 adaptable, <u>bossy</u>, direct, <u>honest</u>, in<u>ventive</u>, <u>passionate</u>, <u>private</u>, <u>stubborn</u>, ad<u>venturous</u>, <u>calm</u>, dog<u>matic</u>, <u>idealistic</u>, <u>jealous</u>, <u>patient</u>, pro<u>tective</u>, <u>trusting</u>, am<u>bitious</u>, <u>careful</u>, dy<u>namic</u>, im<u>pulsive</u>, <u>motivated</u>, <u>playful</u>, re<u>sponsible</u>, <u>warm</u>, <u>balanced</u>, <u>charming</u>, ener<u>getic</u>, in<u>stinctive</u>, <u>open</u>, <u>pompous</u>, <u>secretive</u>, big-<u>hearted</u>, <u>confident</u>, enthu<u>siastic</u>, in<u>tense</u>, op<u>timistic</u>, pos<u>sessive</u>, <u>stable</u>

5 1. open, 2. bossy, 3. dynamic or energetic, 4. intense or passionate, 5. dogmatic, 6. balanced 7. impulsive or instinctive, 8. optimistic, 9. trusting, 10. jealous or possessive

6 1. Pisces, 2. Taurus, 3. Aquarius, 4. Leo, 5. Virgo, 6. Gemini, 7. Scorpio, 8. Cancer, 9. Capricorn, 10. Sagittarius, 11. Libra, 12. Aries

TRACK 10 CD 1

1 1. New Zealand - 2. Norway - 3. Iran - 4. Sicily 5. The Czech Republic - 6. Portugal - 7. Atlanta Hartsfield - 8. Japan - 9. Iceland - 10. Real Madrid

2 1d - 2c - 3a - 4c - 5b - 6d - 7e - 8c - 9a - 10b

3 **One-syllable names:** France, Spain
Stress on first syllable: Cyprus, Finland, Germany, Iceland, Italy, Norway, (New) Zealand, Paraguay, (The) Philippines, Portugal, Sweden, Switzerland
Stress on second syllable: Australia, Iran, Japan, Majorca, Sardinia
Stress on third syllable: Pakistan, Venezuela

4 big / large - small, busy - quiet, cheap - expensive, competitive - uncompetitive, good - bad high - low, generous - mean, quick - slow

5 1. competitive, 2. busy, 3. cheap, 4. expensive/ generous, 5. quiet, 6. high/low, 7. mean, 8. quick

6 1. a) 31/10 b) 10/31 / 2. a) 01/05 b) 05/01 3. a) 20/11/75 b) 11/20/75 / 4. a) 15/08 b) 08/15 5. a) 06/12 b) 12/06 / 6. a) 24/10/29 b) 10/21/29 7. a) 04/07 b) 07/04 / 8. a) 11/09 b) 09/11

7 **One syllable adjectives:** big, cheap, good, high, large, low, quick

Two syllable adjectives: busy
Three (+) syllable adjectives: competitive, expensive, generous

8 ... we put **the** ... and add **-est**
... with the letter **-y**, we put **the** before the adjective, and add **-est**...
... we put **the** and **most** before the adjective.
... we put **the** and **most** before the adjective.

9 1. **the largest** d) Moscow (10.7 million)
2. **the most generous** a) Norway (0.87% of Gross Domestic Product)
3. **the most competitive** a) The USA

10 **What** have you got for dessert?
What flavour have you got?
Which one would you like?
What is straciatella?

TRACK 11 CD 1

1 1. False (Connor wants to hear a song called *The Soul of a man*)
2. True (*Ah yes, I saw that*).
3. True (*Yeah, they were mainly women*).
4. True (*a very small audience*).
5. False (Blues was very influential on British music in the late 60s.)

2 1. the same, 2. 1930, 3. 20th, 4. Race music, 5. electric

3 Preposition: 1, 4, 5, 7, 9 / Verb: 2, 3, 6, 8, 10

4 sadness, loneliness, happiness, blackness, smallness, darkness, lateness, greatness

5 classification, transformation, invasion

6 injustice, incapability, incoherence, incompatibility, inconsistency, inconvenience, independence, indignity, indiscretion, insubordination

7 1. aren't you?, 2. didn't it?, 3. wasn't it? 4. don't you, Connor?, 5. were they?, 6. didn't it?, 7. wasn't it?, 8. was it?, 9. didn't it?

8 1. question, 2. an auxiliary verb, 3. do, 4. affirmative, 5. negative, 6. negative, 7. affirmative

9 1. isn't she?, 2. wasn't it?, 3. did you? 4. doesn't he?, 5. aren't you?, 6. isn't it? 7. was it?, 8. don't we?, 9. do you?, 10. didn't we?

10 Ascendente: 3 / Descendente: 1, 2, 4

11 1. This opera **was written** by Guiseppe Verdi in 1871. / 2. Five houses **were destroyed** by the fire. / 3. The conference **will be opened** by the President of the USA. / 4. The ozone layer **is being destroyed** (by us). / 5. The 2008 Formula 1 world championship **was won** by Lewis Hamilton. / 6. Photos of Madonna's wedding to Guy Ritchie **were published** by *The Mail*. / 7. The United Nations **was criticised** for not preventing the massacre of civilians. / 8. The Sagrada Familia **was designed** by Antoni Gaudí. / 9. Some excellent wine **is made** in Chile. / 10. 5,000 litres of beer **were drunk** by visitors to the event.

TRACK 12 CD 1

1 1. a stereo, 2. an electric guitar 3. a kid's bike, 4. an adult's bike 5. a laptop computer, 6. a motorbike, 7. a cat with kittens, 8. an acoustic guitar, 9. a home studio, 10. a mobile phone

2 **Caller 1:** a laptop computer / € 400
Caller 2: two adult's bikes / € 500 for one € 800 for two
Caller 3: four kittens / nothing
Caller 4: a mobile phone / € 100
Caller 5: a home studio, an electric guitar / € 750

3 1. a laptop computer. / Yes, perfectly. / He got a better one for his birthday. / 666 54 99 49.
2. two bicycles for adults / Three years. / No space in her new apartment. / 647 50 50 17
3. four kittens / black and white / Hasn't got enough space for them. / chrisdalaras@hotmail.com
4. mobile phone / Nokia, latest model / Going back to Scotland, can't use it there. / 655 83 52 68
5. electric guitar, home recording studio/equipment. / No. / Making some space, changing her life. / barbara70@yahoo.com

4 1. ... so I'm **try**ing to sell **this** one **now**.
2. How **much** are you **ask**ing for it?
3. Right, that's **Steve**, who's **sell**ing a **lap**top com**pu**ter and he's **ask**ing € **400** for it.
4. **Why** are you **sell**ing them, if I can **ask**?
5. Go a**head**, Chris, **what are you** trying to **sell**?

5 bought, give away, sold, buy, buy, bought, sell, bought

6 happening now, as we speak.
1. 6, 2. 6, 3. 6, 4. 6, 5. 7

7 1. is wearing, 2. is having, 3. go, 4. are you staying, 5. are losing, 6. play, 7. am watching 8. is going, 9. spend, 10. go

8 1 b, 2 b, 3 a, 4 a, 5 a, 6 b, 7 a, 8 a, 9 a, 10 a

TRACK 01 CD 2

1 1. She's a wedding organiser/planner.
2. At a software company. / 3. Patience, organisation, good negotiation skills, quick and resolute in difficult moments, have good communication skills. / 4. Because they work so much and don't have time. / 5. People are less patient than they were before. / They don't make an effort when things go wrong.

2 1. Her bouquet of flowers. / 2. At least 12. / 3. By Internet / They do an internet search and leave her a message. / 4. To get the best suppliers for the best prices. / 5. Good communication with your partner.

4 1 b, 2 b, 3 c, 4 b, 5 b, 6 a, 7 d, 8 a

TRACK 02 ◀ CD 2

1 Juliet: 1 c, 2 c / Sue: 1 a, 2 b / Stuart: 1 a, 2 c

2 **Juliet:** 1. True, 2. True, 3. False (for two years)
Sue: 1. False (28 boys to every girl), 2. True, 3. False (they didn't talk)
Stuart: 1. True, 2. False (they broke up when they went to university), 3. False (he got married in Bali)

3 1 d, 2 e, 3 a, 4 g, 5 b, 6 c, 7 j, 8 k, 9 f, 10 i, 11 h

4 **Regular verbs:** asked somebody out, chatted somebody up, kissed, moved in, stayed together
Irregular verbs: broke up, broke somebody's heart, fell in love, got married, made eye contact, were together

5 *Suggested answer:* 1. they made eye contact, 2. he/she chatted him/her up, 3. he/she asked him/her out, 4. they kissed, 5. they fell in love, 6. they moved in together, 7. they got engaged, 8. they got married, 9. he/she broke his/her heart, 10. they broke up

7 1 d, 2 c, 3 f, 4 h, 5 a, 6 c, 7 e, 8 g

8 1. the love of my life, 2. chat me up, 3. ask him out, 4. partner, 5. break up, 6. fell in love, 7. get married, 8. couples, 9. broke my heart, 10. kiss

TRACK 03 ◀ CD 2

1 **Lewis:** 5, 6 / **Liam:** 2, 3, 4 / **Both:** 1, 7, 8

2 1. False (his mother does), 2. True, 3. False (his younger brother), 4. True, 5. False (they let him go)

3 fazer as pazes make up, pegar pick up, dar-se bem get on with, sair go out, acabar fazendo alguma coisa end up, ficar de fora stay out

4 1. Correct, 2. Incorrect (go out tonight), 3. Incorrect (get on well with your parents), 4. Correct, 5. Incorrect (ended up living), 6. Correct

6 **Lewis:** usually, usually
Liam: usually, usually, always, always

7 never, hardly ever, quite often, generally/usually, always / Os advérbios de frequência normalmente ficam entre o sujeito e o verbo.

TRACK 04 ◀ CD 2

1 1. a) True, b) True, c) False (four years ago)
2. a) True, b) True, c) False (the 70s), c) False (in Australia)

3. a) False (in church), b) True, c) True
4. a) True, b) False (doesn't say that), c) True

2 1. He moved to London.
2. He started writing his own songs.
3. He started playing with his present group.

3 1. blues, classical, country, flamenco, pop / 2. 12-13

4 1. funny, 2. fun, 3. funny, 4. funny, 5. fun, 6. fun, 7. funny, 8. funny, 9. funny, 10. fun

5 So how many albums **have you made**?
I've made five, so far, but-.
(...) **I've written** seven songs for it, m

6 been, begun, come, drunk, driven, eaten, given, had, known, made, seen, spoken, taken, written

7 1. I've bought, 2. I saw, 3. Have you ever tried / haven't, 4. has made, 5. won, 6. did you go, 7. I've seen, 8. went up, 9. has lost, 10. didn't visit

8 How long **have you been singing**?
Singing? I suppose **I've been singing** since...

9 1. been living, 2. been studying, 3. been looking for, 4. been driving, 5. been trying, 6. been playing, 7. been going, 8. been learning, 9. been growing, 10. been watching

10 Well, for the **past** four **years** I've **work**ed with the same mu**sic**ians.
How long have you been **sing**ing?
I sup**pose** I've been **sing**ing since I was a **boy**.
I **like** just about **ev**ery**thing**, but I've **nev**er really liked instru**ment**al jazz.
So **how** many **al**bums have you **made**?
I've **writ**ten **sev**en songs for it.

TRACK 05 ◀ CD 2

1 1. a) autumn-winter, b) women / 2. a) brighter, b) Asian, c) strong, d) 33%, e) will not be

2 1. False (she says he is, even if he doesn't know it), 2. False (18-35) 3, 4, 5. True

3 1. Juliet, 2. Stuart, 3. Sue, 4. Stuart, 5. Juliet

4 amarelo yellow, azul blue, branco white, cinza grey, marrom brown, roxo purple, preto black, vermelho red, rosa pink, verde green

5 botas boots, calças trousers, sutiã bra, camiseta T-shirt, saia skirt, suéter jersey, sapatos shoes, blusa blouse, camisa shirt, meias socks, calcinhas panties, vestido dress, cueca underpants, calça leggings

1ª edição fevereiro de 2011 | **Diagramação** Patrícia De Michelis
Fonte Zine Slab e Zine Sans | **Papel** Offset 75g/m²
Impressão e acabamento Yangraf